The Horse
Who Loved Picnics

The Horse Who Loved Picnics

by Sandy Dengler

MOODY PRESS

CHICAGO

ISBN: 0-8024-3589-0

Contents

CHAPTER   PAGE

1. Carrie's Cross to Bear   7
2. The Fleece That Fell Over   21
3. The Fleece Flies High   39
4. Barn Fire!   53
5. Mr. Hostetler's Drastic Measures   75
6. Chet Disappears   93
7. Roller Finds a Picnic   105

1

Carrie's Cross to Bear

In Springer, Texas, at four o'clock, the place to be was Grant's Mercantile. An iron wood-burning stove (more properly, a box heater) sat in a tray of sand in the middle of the floor. Around the stove sat a half dozen chairs in various states of partial collapse. And in late afternoon all the farmers stopped by Grant's for a cup of Mrs. Grant's coffee and a few words with the neighbors before they left town.

Daniel had never sat on one of those rickety chairs. By unwritten law, the oldest farmers got the choice of seats, and by 3:00 P.M. or so there were always more men than chairs. Even Pop was sitting on the floor today, hunkered down beside Daniel, with his elbows on his knees.

To Pop's right, Caleb Bennett scrunched down and stretched out his legs. His chair creaked ominously. "Out on my spread hit's so dry the jackrabbits rattle when they hop."

Another nodded. "I hear Wesmorton's cattle are so skinny he's branding 'em two at a time with carbon paper."

"Had to pin the stamp to that letter I sent last week. Ain't had no spit to spare since September."

"Our milk cow's flanks are so sunk in they meet at the middle."

"You think *your* cow's poorly—we gotta prime ours like a pump before she'll give any milk at all."

"Found a piece o' wire out behind the shed Saddiddy." Sam Watson scratched his beard. "Didn't know what it might be from. Hit seemed in good shape as wire goes—nice and straight—except it was all loose at one end. So I used it to make a bale for Ma's bucket. But she left it soaking in the washtub all night, and the next morning I heard her screaming. That wire had soaked up water and puffed out to what it had been before it dried out—a rattlesnake. I thought that was a mighty loose end on it."

Daniel found it terribly hard to keep from laughing. But it seemed to be a general rule that nobody laughed. People might smile a bit or snort—which was a giggle of sorts. But there was no laughing.

"Sure wish it would rain in the next couple years," drawled Porter Webster. "Not so much for me, y'know. I've seen rain before. But my son ain't."

"You mean Gemmy ain't never seen rain?"

"Who's talkin' 'bout Gemmy? I mean Dale—the one who's married and got two kids."

Pop stood up and stretched, so Daniel stood up too.

"Dan, guess we best go home and start taking the house apart."

"Taking the house apart?"

"Gonna try wringing water out of the adobe bricks. I know for a fact there was water in 'm when I mixed the clay three years ago."

Daniel felt his face turn just a wee bit red. His own pop had laid the trap, and he had fallen for it! They said good-bye all around and walked outdoors into the dusty Springer street.

Daniel loved coming to town with Pop like this, just the two of them. Although he was just thirteen, Pop treated him like a man. He never said, "Wait outside," or "Stay in the wagon." Even when he talked to the bank manager about a loan, Daniel stood beside him.

Daniel climbed into the wagon box as Pop

untied Caesar and Cleopatra. He clambered in, Daniel glanced behind them, and the team lurched forward into the street. Caesar and Cleo knew the way home. All Daniel needed to do was keep them from colliding with some other farmer's homebound rig.

They passed the last of the mud-brick buildings and the stockyard. Straight, empty road stretched out ahead. They had dropped off Mom at Carsons' that morning, so they would stop to pick her up now. Pop reached under the seat and pulled out the hemp rope that would be Lumpy the Cow's new tether. He groped again, found his pointed stick, and commenced unraveling the rope end.

Out on the flats beyond, a twenty-foot funnel of dust picked up. It scudded across the bare, dry dirt, getting thicker. Finally it hit a creosote bush and exploded into nothing. Daniel counted three such dust devils out across the flat. No, four.

"I was talking to Caleb Bennett quite a while today," mused Pop. "He says a dry year like this is normal. In fact, 1879 was unusually wet, he says."

"That's when we came to Texas. And I thought it looked dry then. You know, Pop, I remember seeing grass then where I've never seen grass since then. Like down by the hobnail cliffs."

10

Daniel could also remember how green Illinois looked nearly any time, but he did not say so. Illinois was past, three years ago. His friends there had surely changed; in fact, they had probably forgotten him. He had new friends now and more responsibilities. And he had Jesus. His life in Texas was so totally different from his childhood back in Illinois that he could not even compare them. Just the fact that he was thirteen changed his whole existence, for now he was nearly a man.

Out of his pocket Pop fished the honda he had purchased at the hardware store. He wrapped the end of the rope around it, measuring by eye. He pushed his pointed stick into the rope, twisted it open, and forced in one of the raveled ends. Pop could splice a honda into a loop quicker and tighter than anyone else Daniel knew.

"Pop, what was Mom talking about Lumpy coming fresh?"

"Wants to bring off a calf next year. You see, a cow has to bear a calf every year or so or she'll quit giving milk. So I opine we'll take Lumpy over to Will Peterson's this next month and introduce her to Good Time Charlie."

"Why not Wesmorton?"

"Wes runs beef cattle, Dan. Only got one little milk cow on his whole place—and he bought 'r from Will. Will owns a first class dairy bull."

"Good Time Charlie is his bull?"

"Nice a bull as any I ever saw, even back in Illinois."

Daniel grinned. "You been thinking about Illinois, too, huh?"

Pop looked at him. "You still miss back East?"

"Sorta. Some ways. I like it out here, too."

Pop nodded. "Me, too. Some days I wish we were still there. The reason we left was taxes, mostly, and being hemmed in. Our place was too small to live off of, but we couldn't buy more land with prices so high. Out here we got all the space in the world. No water to green it up at all, but all the space in the world."

"Might we ever go back to Illinois?"

"Can't. We sold our place outright, for cash. Used some of the money to move out here. Used more that first year, building this place, meeting homestead requirements. Had to buy seed three times instead of once, what with the javelinas* eating the beans and the cotton drying up. Now we don't have enough money to move that far, let alone buy another place."

"We're stuck here, then, in West Texas."

"Here or somewhere else out here. Hank Carson heard about green valleys and good

*Hah-vah-LEE-na—the peccary, or wild pig.

12

climate over in Arizona."

"I thought Arizona was all cactus worse'n this."

"So'd I. 'Course, you can't believe every rumor you hear. Hank was just talking, passing on what he heard."

"Well, we got enough money this year. I heard you say so."

Pop licked his lips. He seemed uncertain whether to say what was on his mind. Suddenly he shrugged. "You're practically grown up, Dan. We consider you another man in the family, really. So I'll tell you what Mom and I know. There's money for maybe one planting. We had enough for three and then some until the girls got sick. Doctor took a chunk and the medicine another chunk. Understand I'm not complaining. I don't begrudge the girls all the money in the world and I daresay it saved Grace's life. But we're about to the bottom of the barrel again."

Saved Grace's life. Daniel did not even like to think about the scarlet fever. Nobody knew why Daniel and Naomi, the four-year-old, had not come down with it. But then, nobody knew why eleven-year-old Grace and nine-year-old Rachel had. It looked like Rachel was the only one for a while, until Grace threw up as she walked across the kitchen—as big a surprise to her as to anyone else.

13

Then came the days of rashes and fevers, the weird color of the girls' tongues, like ripe strawberries; Mom taking turns all day and all night rocking first one quilt-wrapped girl and then the other. Daniel washed dishes and clothes, Pop cooked and ironed, and neither one complained. They worked together as a team, just as they did gathering cordwood, splitting rails, or drenching Caesar.

Daniel thought about Chet's family and how none of them wanted to do a lick more work than necessary (except maybe Chet and his ma). They did not pull together as a team like Daniel's family or the Carsons did. But then Chet was the only Hollis who was a Christian. Did that have anything to do with it? Maybe not. Daniel's family had worked together before they were saved, too. It was a confusing thought.

They rattled into the Carson yard at suppertime. Daniel set the brake, and Pop tied up Cleo. He got together with Mr. Carson.

"Got everything on your list, Hank, but you forgot to say how many eight-penny nails. So I bought two pounds."

"That'll do fine. Your wife's got supper waiting. She made a rib roast that's nothing short of elegant. Showed Carrie how to make strudel, too."

"Strudel! Yippee!" Daniel hustled into the

14

house, the better to sniff the aroma of his favorite dessert.

Clifford and Rachel were in the way, as usual, sprawled on the hall rug, playing jacks.

Daniel liked the way the Carson family was a sort of inside-out version of his own. He and Carrie were the same age within a month. Cliff and Rachel were within six months of each other, both coming ten. Of course, the pattern fell apart then, because Matt was two years older than Daniel, and Royal was two years older than Naomi. But still, the balance was interesting.

Daniel slipped into the kitchen and took an inconspicuous place near the strudel. Usually, any room Mom was in bubbled over with warmth. This kitchen was absolutely glum.

Mom paused to smile at him, but it was a vacant sort of smile. "Good. You two are here. Carrie, you might go tell your ma dinner's ready."

"Yes'm. H'lo, Dan." Her smile was cheerless, too. She disappeared out the door.

"What's wrong, Mom? You and Mrs. Carson get in a fight or something?"

"Not at all. In fact, all the talking and visiting wore her out. She's napping. Go tell the men to come. And on your way out take this tub of grease drippings. While I'm making soap tomorrow I might as well pour off a batch for Clara, too."

The tub was heavy. It was a good thing it did not slosh. Daniel yelled at Rachel to get out of the way and asked Cliff to open the door. He trotted down off the porch a bit faster than he intended. The tub thunked down on the tailgate so hard the wagon bounced. Then he whistled the special whistle he and Pop used to call each other to dinner.

Matt came around the corner from the woodshed, smiling another one of those vacant smiles. "H'lo, Dan." He went inside.

Here came Pop and Mr. Carson, both grim, both quiet.

Daniel's chest was starting to flutter. "Pop? What's going on around here?"

"Carsons are moving to Arizona next month."

"You know Clara's not well, Dan," said Mr. Carson. Daniel knew that. Mrs. Carson was always having nervous fits of one sort or another. "We hope the new area—an area she maybe will like better than Texas—will do her some good."

Pop wrapped his arm around Daniel's shoulder and turned him toward the house. They walked together, matching strides. "You see, Dan, Hank figures with the mining out there—gold, copper—there's bound to be a good market for farm produce. Arizona's filling up with miners, prospectors, schemers—lots of people who have to eat."

"But it's so—so far."

"Very nearly as far as Illinois."

Very nearly as far as Illinois. And Illinois seemed a whole world away. During the next hour they washed up, ate dinner, and sat out on the porch for tea and conversation—and not a bit of it registered with Daniel.

Carsons moving. If anyone could make a go of it here on the riverbottom, it was Carsons. They were the only ones showing a profit. Mr. Carson even turned his hay into a cash crop this year, selling it at top price to ranchers and stablemen.

Carsons moving. They would disappear from Daniel's life—Matt, Carrie, all of them—and find new friends a thousand miles away. Carrie was one of the few people Daniel really enjoyed being with. And then, he depended upon Matt a lot whenever he needed some spiritual question answered.

Carsons moving.

Clumsy Brunhilde, wrapped in a tan hide three sizes too large for her, waddled over to Daniel and plopped her head in his lap. Obviously she was due to produce another litter of pups soon. The Carsons even made a little money selling her pups. Big, amiable, depend-

17

able farm dogs were hard to find. Brunny, even taking all her extra skin into account, was huge. In addition, her herding know-how made her an excellent drover's dog for handling livestock. And she passed on that skill to her pups. She stuck her doggy face into his and licked his ear. Daniel did not mind.

Carrie lifted the sock she had been darning and gave it a jerk. The hard-boiled goose egg dropped out the bottom. She put egg and needle in her sewing basket, stood up, and stretched. She did a woman's work. Everybody said so. "Rosie hasn't been milked yet. I better do that before it gets any darker." She started off across the yard toward the cow shed.

Daniel shoved Brunny aside and ran to catch up. "Need help watching the milk foam up?"

"Sure do. That's one of the hardest parts of milking. That and drying your hands off when you're through."

Carrie milked Rosita like Mom milked Lumpy. She talked to the little cow, scratched her behind the horns and under the neck, hand-fed her a piece of carrot. When she washed off Rosita's udder with cold water and started working, the milk came down right away—thin and pearly, then white and foamy, and finally so creamy it was almost yellow.

As he had promised, Daniel watched the foam creep up the pail. When he and Carrie were together like this they did not always talk a blue streak. Sometimes they just hung around, together and yet alone, each in his own thoughts. In a way, Daniel liked that much better than talking. Melanie Hawes giggled at school and sang, "Danny has a girl friend," now and then. But Melanie Hawes was a silly goose anyway.

As soon as Carrie stood up and took away the pail, Daniel untied Rosita and forked clean hay into her manger. Carrie hung up the manure shovel, and Daniel reached for the milk pail. Pop said you must always be a gentleman, so that meant carrying her pail for her. Carrie's cheeks were wet. She glanced up at him, ashamed, and turned away.

Now what should he do? When his little sisters cried it did not bother him a bit, but this was something else. He leaned on the doorway so close he was almost touching her.

"You don't want to leave, do you?"

"No. Dan, it's a sin to say so, but I'm so sick and tired of Ma being like she is. I'm sick of being stuck with all the housework and cooking while she sits and does something useless—or nothing at all. She lies in bed with a headache for days at a time, and I'm so sick of making Royal behave, and—" Carrie was crying in earnest now. The sobbing made her voice stuttery. "And now we have to move be-

19

cause of her. The only two things I want is to stay here and to go to school. And I can't have either one. And all because of her."

She was right. It just wasn't fair. And Daniel could not see that it was sin to say so out loud, either. Truth is truth. He had felt helpless on occasion, not knowing what to do, but never like this. Since there was nothing he could think of to do, he just stood and held onto her while she cried on his shoulder.

It was all so painfully unfair. And he could not do a thing about it.

2

The Fleece
That Fell Over

Pop bounced through the kitchen door and
whumped down in his chair. Mom scooped hot
cakes and bacon off the griddle onto his plate.
He poured syrup as he talked. "Morning, Dan.
How's school?"

"Pretty good, except Mr. Devlin giving me a
pile of homework lately."

"Good. Fine. Couldn't happen to a nicer
kid."

"Pop, ever think of moving to Arizona?"

"Yep. Forget it."

"Oh." Daniel pushed at his breakfast with
his fork. That was not the answer he wanted.

Pop continued. "I'd love to. Hank paints a

21

rosy picture of the Arizona river valleys. But frankly, I'm scared to. We don't have much here, but we *have* it. Bird in the hand, you know?"

"And you don't know what's out in the bushes in Arizona."

"Exactly." Pop sipped his coffee. "Got a job for you tomorrow."

There went Saturday. "Sure glad to hear that, Pop. I was worried for a minute I'd have all Saturday off with nothing to do."

"You know I wouldn't let that happen. Grace and I are putting in beans and your Mom's finishing up all that soap. Someone has to go to town, so that means you."

"Go to town with who?"

"With *whom*. Nobody. Just you."

"Sure. Happy to." Daniel filled his mouth with pancakes so that it would be easier to keep from grinning. To town alone! He had never gone to town alone before, much less been trusted with money to buy items on a list. This was grown-up stuff! Daniel rode off to school in a heady cloud of joy.

The Carson boys arrived at the crossroads the same time the Tremains did. The three boys were pressed together on their horse, arms around waists, just as Daniel and his sisters were packed onto Caesar's back.

"Where's Carrie, Matt?"

"She had to quit early. Since we're moving and there's so much to do, Pa thought she ought. I'll quit, too, in a couple more weeks."

Daniel's heart, so light and happy a moment ago, fell with a thump. Carrie would not even be at school anymore. And she wanted to so much.

"That's too bad. For Carrie, I mean."

"I'll help her at home—help tutor her. She won't miss out too much."

It's not the same, Daniel thought. *Not the same to her or anyone else.* But he did not say so. He did not tell Matt about going to town alone tomorrow, either. Almost fifteen, Matt often went to town alone, so it was no big thing for him.

The horses plodded along beside each other.

"Matt, how'd your father decide to move?"

"Put out a couple fleeces and that's the way the dew fell."

"Huh?"

"You read Judges yet?"

"No. I'm still in the New Testament."

"All right. In the book of Judges, a man named Gideon was called to lead the Israelites in war. He was afraid, so he put out a fleece—I mean a real sheep wool—and made a deal with God. If dew fell on the fleece but not the ground, he had read God's signal right and was supposed to go. Next morning he could

23

wring out the fleece, but the ground was bone dry. But he still didn't want to believe it. So he asked God to give him one more sign. This time, the fleece would be dry but the ground would be wet. Well, the next morning it had happened that way. So he went."

"Hard to convince, huh?"

"Yeah." Matt laughed. "Anyway, to 'put out a fleece' means to set up some situation in order to test whether what you're thinking of doing is what God wants."

"Testing God. I thought Pastor Dougald said not to."

"That kind of testing is different. Testing God is challenging Him for no good reason. Putting out a fleece is—well—asking a question. Making sure of what He wants. See the difference?"

"Mmm." Daniel could, in a way. The idea itself sounded great. Put out the right 'fleece' and there was no way you could miss knowing God's specific intentions in any situation. Daniel would like that kind of certainty—the certainty that would call a successful farmer to leave farm and friends behind and travel seven hundred miles into the unknown.

He thought about fleeces all day. At noon he asked Matt for the Bible passage—Judges chapter six—and read it for himself. Gideon was such an interesting man he read right on through chapter eight. He could hardly wait for suppertime.

At supper that night Daniel had to wait halfway through the meal until Grace ran out of school incidents and rumors to tell. Finally Pop just told her to stop talking and eat.

"Pop, I was reading about fleeces today."

"If you plan to run sheep here in cattle country, you got trouble coming."

"Spiritual fleeces."

"Didn't know there were any. Keep angels warm in winter?"

"It's a situation you set up in order to find out what God wants you to do exactly. If this happens, He wants such-and-so. If that happens, He doesn't. It's in Judges. About Gideon."

"I see what you mean." Mom nodded. Daniel realized she must have read that by now. She had started reading the Bible not with Matthew but with Genesis. "See how the dew falls."

"Exactly. Maybe we ought to set out a fleece of some sort."

Pop snorted. "No dew has fallen here in two years. Too dry. And you'll have to walk to New Mexico to find a fleece."

"You don't need real sheep wool. Any situation will do. I'm thinking we ought to ask God whether He wants us to go to Arizona, too."

"So that's it." Mom reached for a second

helping of mashed potatoes. "What's given you the wanderlust all of a sudden?"

"Well, can we?"

Pop shook his head. "Not as far as I'm concerned. I don't need to ask God about something I have no intention of doing anyway."

"Carsons could use us. It'd be easier for both us families to get started if we went together."

"Dan, we're already started, right here. End of discussion." Pop finished off the potatoes.

End of discussion, all right. Now what? Why did God put into Daniel's head the idea that they ought to go, if He had not put it into Pop's head also? Was the idea from God at all? Might it be Daniel's own notion or even some suggestion from Satan? Was Mr. Carson really acting in God's will? The whole question got more complex and more confusing the more Daniel thought about it.

Most of all he wanted to be near Carrie. Carrie needed someone her age to lean on, and they understood each other. That was very important in view of all the things Carrie was going through, giving up, burdened with. Christians were supposed to help each other, after all.

Mom cut into a prickly-pear pie, her specialty. With sugar and spices she could make a pie of peeled cactus pads taste as good as any apple or rhubarb pie ever did.

Gideon's family didn't put out a fleece; Gideon did, Daniel thought. *Personally. One-to-one with God. Just because Pop doesn't want to doesn't mean I can't.* What should his fleece be?

How about his getting a horse? If they were to live in Arizona he would need a horse. Everyone in Arizona rode a horse (of course, they said that about Texas, too, and Daniel had not really needed one here). No matter. A horse would do nicely. It was not an easy fleece, either. They had no money to buy another horse and no hay to feed one. In fact, there were no horses to buy; no one in the area was selling.

Perfect! If God really wanted the Tremains to go to Arizona, He would provide Daniel with a horse to ride there. Daniel was so pleased with his fleece he almost forgot to ask for a second piece of pie.

The trip into Springer was a marvelous success right from the start. He went to two places besides Grant's to get the best price for the butter and eggs Mom was selling. He spent half an hour comparing nails before he bought any. He even found the right-size lamp chimney to replace the one Naomi had broken. By one o'clock he had purchased everything on

27

Mom's list, and he had $1.65 left over. This going alone into Springer was the greatest thing in the world. He considered dawdling until midafternoon and then spending a few minutes by the stove at Grant's Mercantile, but he could not wait to get home. A dollar sixty-five left over. Wait until Mom saw that.

Daniel assured himself that his purchases were secure under the wagon seat. He climbed into the box, took up the lines, and looked behind him down the street. No one coming. He clucked and slapped the lines across the horses' backs. Nothing moved.

"Caesar! Cleo! Up there!" Daniel rattled the lines.

Caesar sidled nervously, but the horses did not move. Cleopatra tossed his head, and Daniel spied a bright thatch of red hair. Chet Hollis!

Chet stood erect, grinning. He towered head and shoulders above Daniel and was muscular as a blacksmith. But then he was nearly seventeen years old, a man by any measure.

Chet laughed a booming laugh and let go Daniel's horses. "Good to see y', Dan! Leaving already?"

"Got everything done I came to do. How's it going?"

"Mighty fine! Look what I bought me today." Chet dug into his shoulder sack and

28

hauled out a brand new Bible. "They had one with gold edges and this'n with red edges. Figure hit's not the edges, hit's the words inside."

Daniel grinned. "Now I feel bad. I should've bought you one long already."

"Not so! You showed me Jesus. If I care about Him I can spend fifty-five cents buying His Word, right?" Chet stepped in close to the wheel. "Dan, do some praying for me."

"Anything specific?"

"Yeah. I been thinking a long time about leaving home. Tired of doing all the work. But then, what would Ma do without me? And especially, Ma and Pa aren't saved. They won't even listen to me. I want to do what's right—according to what God wants—but for that I gotta know what's right to do."

"You, too, huh?"

"Whaddaya mean?"

Daniel smiled. "Everybody on the riverbottom must be restless. Matt told me about fleeces. Judges six—"

"Where?"

"Gideon set up a plan to find out what God wanted him to do. Like Pop says, we don't have dew or fleece either one, but it's supposed to be a good system. Carsons use it."

Daniel found the place in Chet's new Bible and marked it with a wisp of hay. "It's a way of learning what God wants you to do."

"That's just the thing I need! Thanks, Dan. Say, why not hang around some?"

"Better get home directly. Thanks anyway. Good to see you, Chet. And I'll remember about praying."

"Thanks. Later." Chet grinned and waved.

Daniel pulled out into the street and gave Caesar and Cleopatra an extra little jiggle on the lines. In unison they lurched into a shuffling jog. He recognized Mrs. Fedderson from church and waved to her. His eyes noticed a horse and buggy crossing the street up ahead, but his brain paid no attention.

Suddenly the buggy was parked squarely in front of him! Bracing against the dashboard, Daniel dragged back on the lines for all he was worth. Cleo lunged to the right. Caesar reared up and back and tangled one hind leg in the wagon tongue.

The left front corner of Daniel's wagon crunched into the buggy wheel. Daniel heard wood crack and splinter, but he did not have time to look. Caesar was tangled up in the tugs, and Cleo was trying to kick free and sidle away from the confusion.

A big, burly farmer came running up and grabbed Cleo's bridle. Daniel dropped the lines and pulled open his knife. He jumped the dashboard in front and stood on the tongue to cut Caesar's inside tug. The outside tug was broken already. A couple of other men were at the horses' heads now. Free of the tugs, Caesar pranced a nervous dance as they led him forward and out of the mess.

Daniel released Cleo's tugs, and the big farmer led him off to the nearest hitch rack. Everything had happened so fast. Now that it was about over, Daniel was starting to shake. He ran to Caesar. Another fellow was already running his hands down the horses's legs.

"Lost a little skin inside his hind leg there, but he's fine. You're mightly lucky, son."

Daniel shuddered. "This is luck?"

The man laughed. "Sure is. Why, that buggy stopped in front of you so quick I'm amazed you ducked away in time. You did some fast hauling there, boy."

Another nodded. "Fast thinking, too, cutting your horse free. Ain't you Tremain's kid?"

"Yes, sir." Daniel clicked his knife shut.

"Recognized the team more'n you. You've growed some lately."

Daniel did not know what to say. Was it the wagon that had crunched, or the buggy, or both? He looked over Pop's wagon and could see nothing amiss. No spokes were loose, no boards split. The crunch must have been—yes, it was. The buggy wheel was a shattered wreck. In fact the whole back end was splintered.

Daniel ran around to the front of the buggy.

Its little horse lay fallen in the shafts. Daniel must have knocked the poor thing down. He felt terrible.

And that must be the owner, that shrill little man with gray whiskers and a shabby black coat. A cowboy in a big, floppy hat was holding the fellow's arms and yelling at him. "Won't gain nothing by kicking your horse, mister. Hit weren't his fault!"

The owner wrenched free. "Don't tell me that, bucko! A good buggy ruint, and all acause of that horse! Hit was all account of that horse!" The man turned and saw Daniel. "You! Y' young brat! Hit's all your fault! My buggy's ruint acause of you! Why cain't you watch where you're going?"

Daniel opened his mouth to apologize profusely, but his whole field of vision was suddenly blocked. Chet was here—good old Chet!—and he stepped right in front of Daniel. All Daniel could see was the massive back of Chet's checkered shirt.

Chet's voice rumbled like thunder. "Now, little man, you're gonna quieten, and right away. Daniel here did the best he could to keep from running you down. Better'n most drivers could've. Your buggy didn't just stop dead—it backed right into him. I saw it."

Several other heads nodded. How could such a crowd collect so quickly? Daniel felt like sinking into the ground.

"Nobody's gonna believe that!" the owner shrieked. "Why should I back up out in the middle of the street? You're lying for your friend there. That boy run me down, and he'll pay for my buggy!"

Daniel was thoroughly scared. Pay for a ruined buggy?

Another man squared off beside the owner. "The buggy rolled backwards because your horse dropped, and that's the way he fell. I seen it. If anybody pays anybody, you'll buy this boy two new tugs. That horse o' your'n is too sick and puny to be hauling a buggy. I ain't a man to mollycoddle animals, but what you're doing to that nag's a sin."

A general mutter of agreement floated all around.

The cowboy in the floppy hat had cut the horse free of its shafts. Now he and another fellow were pushing and dragging at the little horse, urging it up. Long moments later, the horse rolled to its belly, paused, jerked onto its front legs, sat and rested, then lunged up onto all four. Its scruffy little nose nearly touched the ground.

The owner was so angry his face was scarlet. "I'll show you stupid softies what I'll do to this horse." He dug into a carpetbag under his buggy seat and dragged out a clumsy, oversize

33

pistol. He marched toward the horse's head. "Hit's my horse, and you namby-pambies can just quit your moaning. Here's the last time he's gonna cost me good money."

"No!" Daniel pushed between the owner and his horse.

The expression on the man's face changed immediately from anger to shrewd calculation. "Maybe you wanna take this horse off my hands, boy."

"How much for him?"

"Ten dollars, and I'm taking a loss."

Daniel's heart fell. "Best I can do is a dollar sixty-five."

"No less'n five."

Daniel fished his money out of his pocket. "This is all I have, right here."

Chet laid a hand on his shoulder. "Now hold on a minute, Dan."

The owner glanced around. He saw no friendly faces. "All right. Just to show I don't hold a grudge for what you did to my buggy—and hit's all your fault!—I'll take a dollar sixty-five for him."

He reached for Daniel's money, but Chet grabbed it first. "Dan's paying you a dollar even, feller. Dan, you'll get a dollar's worth of dog food out of him, and the hide's worth a little something."

"Now hold on! You can't interfere like this!"

But the owner was almost as small as Daniel. His objections did not sound very firm. Confused, Daniel let Chet sort out a dollar for the owner. The rest went back into Daniel's pocket.

The man kept shouting and protesting, getting angrier and angrier, but no one seemed to listen. In fact, the crowd formed a sort of barrier between him and Daniel.

Daniel used a piece of baling wire to mend his tugs. That took ten minutes. Chet, the cowboy, and some others all agreed the little horse could not walk all the way to Daniel's farm, so they ran it up into the wagon on a plank. That took another fifteen minutes. Finally Daniel was hitched up again. With thanks to Chet and the others who had helped, he set off.

He kept looking into the back of the wagon the whole way home. It was real. The nightmare had truly happened. The ragged and feeble little horse stood spraddle-legged in the wagon bed, its nose by Daniel's shoulder. It did not fight. It did not try to jump. It did not act nervous, nor even, it seemed, interested in its fate. It drooped where it had been put, without hope of living or being cared about. Here was the most miserable old animal Daniel had ever seen. And he owned it!

Belatedly he thought of God. He had not stopped to ask God's opinion before he so foolishly offered to buy this scrawny beast. And now he had spent Pop's good money for a worthless animal—worse than worthless, for it would cost more good money to feed. Jesus always prayed before making major decisions. Why, oh, why could Daniel not remember to pray first instead of jumping right in?

The whole family was standing there watching as he drove into the yard a little past suppertime. They could not help but see him coming with that horse up in back. Llorón* came bounding out and fired a variety of barks and yowls at the wagon.

Daniel felt embarrassed. He felt ashamed, too, to have been cheated out of a dollar. It was no less than that—cheated. Pop should have known better than to send a foolish little kid to town on a man's errands.

Daniel dug into his pocket. "Here's the change left, Mom."

She was staring at the horse. "I'm afraid to ask."

"Dog food, according to Chet."

"You mean we own this?" Pop was on the other side of the wagon.

"Yes, sir."

"You didn't pay real money for it, I trust."

Here it comes. Daniel felt his cheeks burn. "A dollar, sir."

"Where'd you get a dollar?" Mom asked.

*Your-OWN—a whiner or crybaby; Daniel's hound.

36

"Your butter and eggs."

"Buy everything on the list?"

"Yes'm."

"Including a lamp chimney?"

"Yes'm."

Mom's voice rose. She was getting excited. "How can you be such a shrewd bargainer and then waste a dollar on this terrible excuse of a horse?"

Daniel would have answered, "Guess I'm just lucky," but he decided this was not the time to be funny.

Pop started to unhitch Caesar and stopped. "Have a little trouble with the tugs there?"

"It's a long story."

"Appears so." Pop sighed deeply. "We'll unload this nag, and you'll scrub down the back of the wagon there. Then come in to supper and tell us about it."

"I don't think he'll back off without a ramp."

"He'll get off." Pop threw a rope over the horse's swayed neck and wrapped the other end around Caesar's hames. He walked Caesar away, and the little horse came down off the back of the wagon all in a heap. Daniel did not say anything. He could tell Pop was angry enough to spit nails. Pop's quiet-mad was worse than his yelling-mad.

The little horse struggled to its feet, and Pop threw the rope to Daniel. "Grace, Rachel, put the horses up. Dan, I'm not going to spend a single penny or a single minute of my time on this horse. It's your horse; it's your responsibility. And I want my dollar back sooner or later. So you can just work it out any way you see fit. Not a penny, not a minute." Pop walked off into the house.

Daniel stood there a long time with his horse, just looking at it. He noted its height—short, almost pony size. It was long in the flanks, which meant a poor keeper—a horse that would eat and eat and never gain weight. He would probably call its color grulla.† The mix of black, dark brown, and yellow hairs made it look even dirtier than it was. The hair would not lay flat and gave the horse a lackluster appearance. The head was too big, the rump end too small. The breast and barrel were so narrow that its legs nearly met in front. There was not a spare ounce of meat anywhere. "Skin and bones" was most appropriate. Except for the bloated belly, skin and bones were all you could see.

How much feed would it take to strengthen this pony to where it could walk, let alone fatten it? What if it just dropped over first?

With Llorón bouncing and barking alongside, Daniel led his new horse to the barn under a heavy cloud of gloom.

---

†GROO-ya—a dark smoky brown with light, brassy flanks and belly.

3

The Fleece Flies
High

Sunday morning Daniel picketed his horse out in the greenest part of the farm—the grassy patch by the mesquites in the front yard. By the time they returned from church the pony had the grass all clipped short. He stood in the shade half asleep, his lower lip hanging loose.

Daniel turned Caesar and Cleopatra out into the corral. The girls spread a picnic cloth by the springhouse. Everyone agreed it was too hot in the house to eat inside. Mom brought out the chicken stew with dumplings, and Pop carried the glass lemonade pitcher because Rachel might have dropped it.

Daniel enjoyed eating outside. One did not have to watch manners so carefully. Grace returned from shutting up Llorón in the woodshed (the dog made himself unwelcome at picnics by begging and stealing). They commenced eating as soon as Pop said grace. Food gets cool quickly outside.

Suddenly Grace started laughing so hard she swallowed her milk backwards and choked. She coughed and sputtered and tried to speak. Rachel and Naomi started giggling, and Pop had a bemused "what's happening?" look on his face. They were all looking not at Daniel, but beyond him. Daniel turned to look and jumped two inches. He sat nose to nose with his horse. The grulla had joined their picnic.

"How did he get loose?" asked Mom.

Daniel drew in the tether rope. "The stake came out of the ground, I guess. It's still tied to the other end of the rope here."

Pop turned the stake over in his hand. "Came out, my foot. Your horse grabbed it in his teeth and pulled it out. Here's the marks."

"Aw, Pop, he couldn't be that smart."

"He may look stupid, but he knows a thing or two about picket pins. You're going to have to have to tie him to something permanent from now on—a tree or bush or something."

Daniel fished a piece of carrot out of his

chicken stew and offered it on the palm of his hand. The horse lipped it up. How about a couple of green beans? The grulla accepted.

"Dan—" his Mom warned.

Daniel knew no one was permitted to feed the dog from the table. The horse would naturally be included in the ban.

"Yes'm."

But he did not take the horse back, not just then. In the first place, they had been gone for hours. Why did the horse not pull up its stake and wander off earlier, inasmuch as it obviously knew how? Why wait until now, when people were eating a picnic dinner?

Lonely. The little horse was lonely. That must be it. Daniel would have to give him more attention.

The next Sunday, Rachel wanted to eat dinner out on the high spot beyond the barn. From there you could barely see a bit of the river winding in the distance. The scarp on the Mexico side shimmered blue-buff in the dry heat of midafternoon. Daniel started buttering his cornbread the moment Pop finished saying grace.

Pop glanced toward the house. "If that don't beat all!"

Daniel looked back. The grulla was coming toward them at a trot, the fastest pace Daniel had ever seen him muster. It was a rolling, wallowing sort of trot. The grulla's body rocked sideways as it moved, and it was moving fast, too.

"Dan, where'd you have him?"

"In the corral with Caesar and Cleo."

The grulla slowed to a walk, its feet stirring clouds of dust. It stood behind Daniel, expectant.

Mom scowled. "You give him any of your sweet potatoes or cornbread, and you don't get seconds. Hear me?"

Pop sighed and stood up. "If he's out, Caesar and Cleo must be, too. Rachel, you were the last one through the corral gate. You can just come help me put them back in. Come on, cayuse." He took the grulla by the chin and ear to lead him off. The little horse snapped his head back and ducked away.

"He's lonesome, Pop. Mightn't he stay? I'll bring him in then."

"Ridiculous." But Pop walked off without him.

Daniel glanced at Mom. She was studying the grulla with a new look in her eye, one of interest and maybe even appreciation. "Know what you have there, Dan? A pacing mustang."

"I wasn't keeping track of his feet. I didn't see. A natural pacer, huh? That's why he rocks back and forth like that as he comes."

"What's a pacing?" asked Naomi. "Does that mean there's even more wrong with his horse?"

Mom laughed. "It's the way he moves, Button. When your average horse trots, a front leg and its opposite hind leg hit the ground at the same time. Near fore with off hind, off fore with near hind. But a pacer doesn't trot. The two near feet hit the ground together, then the two off feet."

Grace's brow puckered. "Let's see. If you're looking at him from the left side, his two left feet would swing forward at once, and then the two right feet—horribly uncomfortable to try to ride him!"

"On the contrary," said Mom. "A natural pacer gives a smooth, easy ride, once you're used to it. Smoother than a trot. If you don't start eating while you think, Dan, your dinner is going to freeze solid."

"I got his name, Mom, just now. Easy Roller. From the smooth way he moves."

Naomi looked puzzled. "But Grace says his name is That Old Crowbait."

"I did not!" Grace protested. She glanced at Mom. "Not exactly."

"Easy Roller." A perfect name.

Pop and Rachel came jogging up. She was snuffling and her eyes were wet. Mom looked at Pop for an explanation.

43

Pop plopped down in his place. "She claims she closed the gate up tight, but there it was hanging wide open. She's miffed at me because I pointed out the evidence to the contrary."

"Because he won't believe me! I *did* close the gate right."

"All right," said Mom, "we've heard both sides. Now eat your dinner, Rachel, and be extra careful next time."

"You don't believe me either." Rachel sat and sulked the whole meal. When Mom finally excused her from eating her sweet potatoes, Daniel gave them to his horse.

"Roller is ready to ride. I'm sure of it." Daniel hung over the corral rail watching his little grulla flick flies. Roller could by no stretch of the imagination be called plump. But he had filled out enough that he did not look quite ready to drop anymore. He shook his shaggy head. The flies were starting early this year.

"Yep, he's ready. Today's the day, Grace."

Beside him, Grace snorted and brushed stray hair out of her eyes. "So you want a medal or something? How about a party? Gifts and a cake with one candle. Let's celebrate."

"Who put the burr under your tail today?"

"You and that stupid horse. Roller is this. Roller is that. I'm sick of hearing about your

44

stupid old horse."

"Then why are you standing here admiring him?"

"Admiring?! That bag of bones?"

"You're just jealous because he's prettier 'n you." Daniel turned his back on his squawking, sputtering sister and went to the barn for his new bosal.*

Last Saturday he had spent nearly a whole day up at the Guirrans' ranch. Dos very patiently showed him how to braid a rope bosal over a rawhide base. In a way it was good that Daniel did not have a bridle or the money to buy one. This bosal was even nicer than the bridle would have been. Roller's blanket was the baby blanket Naomi had outgrown. It would do nicely—until he could afford one of those fancy woven wool saddle rugs.

Proudly he strode out to the corral and skinned through the rails. Roller watched him coming and flicked an ear. Daniel slipped the basal on the pony's nose and dragged the headstall up behind his ears. It fit perfectly. And didn't it look handsome! He folded the blanket across the grulla's back and led him over to the fence.

Grace hung over the top rail, heckling.

---

*Boh-sl—a bridle that uses a stiff loop over the horse's nose instead of a bit in its mouth. The reins join in a big knot under the horse's chin.

Daniel would take it easy for this first time. He put his foot on the second rail up and gently boosted himself aboard. Roller ducked his head down. Daniel was not exactly certain what happened next. It seemed as though Roller simply came apart in the middle and dropped Daniel in the dirt. When he sat up, Roller was standing on the far side of the corral. And Grace was running toward the house shrieking for Mom.

He must have slipped getting on. He led Roller back to the rails and climbed on again, more carefully this time. The braided reins ripped from his hand as Roller's head went down. Daniel managed to stay on for two bucks. Then he was in the air a bit higher than the top rail. Free flight is an exhilarating feeling, in a way. He did not remember coming down.

Mom held him tightly, a hand gripping each shoulder. Her face was the color of old ashes. He must not have fallen badly—he was standing up. They were outside the corral. Roller stood half asleep inside the rails. twitching flies.

"Dan?"

"Mom, he bucked me off. Roller pitched me!"

"You don't say. Look at me." She stared him in the eye, so he stared back. She sighed and

46

stood up straight. "Well, at least your eyes can focus now. Come on in the house and sit down. Where are you going? No!"

"I have to go take his bosal off, Mom."

"Later. Come in the house."

"But Mom—"

She took his elbow and steered him toward the kitchen door. She probably knew best. He felt awfully wobbly. It would be good just to sit awhile and think about what to do next. He noticed Grace for the first time, bobbing alongside.

Grace burbled, "Roller threw you clean outta the corral, Dan! You shoulda seen yourself! Mom and I were on the porch when you came sailing up over the top rail and *splat*!" She slapped her hands together smartly. "Did you ever look funny!"

"Funny? Hardly!" Mom snorted. She pushed Daniel into the kitchen ahead of her. He plopped into a chair. She poured him a glass of milk and spooned lots of molasses into it. She fixed herself a cup of tea and sagged wearily into the chair across from him, watching him, acting as if she expected him to explode or drop over or something else.

How could something so great go so wrong? Daniel did not even want to think about Roller. So he thought about Mom instead and how her tea had changed with the years.

Back in Illinois Mom had been the daughter of a wealthy family. When Daniel was little, she dressed elegantly, even though Pop was just a small dirt farmer. And her tea times were equally elegant. She would measure the tea leaves, heat her china tea pot, and steep her tea according to a little timer made like an hourglass. She would pour tea through a strainer, serving her guests (if any) by some invisible rank Daniel could never figure out.

But the elegant dresses faded with time. The hems grew ragged, the cuffs and sleeves stained dark. Elegance was replaced by plain calicos (actually, Daniel liked her much better in calico—she looked warmer, more motherly). And the tea, once so carefully and properly prepared, went the way of other elegance. Now she made tea Pop's way. She pinched a few leaves directly into her cup, poured in hot water, stared at it a minute or two while the color darkened; and that was tea. She rarely bothered to strain it. "That's what front teeth are for," she said. "That's what a moustache is for," said Pop.

Daniel was getting stiff. His body ached all over, mostly up around his shoulders. Roller.

"Mom, Roller's broke. How could he do that to me?"

"Broke to harness. But is he broke to ride?"

"Why would anyone train a horse to harness

48

and not bother to saddle break him as well?"

"Apparently someone did."

"What am I gonna do?"

"I don't know. I do know you're not going to get on that horse again. We'll ask your father. He's hilling potatoes with the girls, so he'll come home to lunch early, I suspect."

Grace suddenly ran outside. The kitchen door slammed *whanck*! Mom closed her eyes. She told the children a dozen times a day not to do that.

"Guess Pop's home, Mom. The town crier just went out to give him the news."

Pop came through the door (*whanck* again) as Daniel was draining the last of his milk. Pop threw the bosal over on the woodbox and stretched out in his chair. Mom set a teacup in front of him and poured.

He grinned. "When man learns to fly, Dan, you'll be up there leading the flock."

"That's not funny, Ira." Mom sat down. "That little horse nearly killed him."

Pop scratched his moustache, then scratched behind his ears. "How's he get along with Cleopatra?"

"Better than with Caesar." Daniel shrugged. The shrug was a mistake. His shoulders hurt too much.

"Let's go put the tongue on the wagon and harness Roller in with Cleo." Pop headed out the door with his teacup in his hand. Daniel knew Mom hated to have people take her dishes outside like that. Mom surely was suffering through a lot this morning.

Roller did not object in the slightest as Pop and Daniel harnessed him. They shortened Caesar's bridle as much as possible but the bit still hung low in his mouth. Pop hopped up in the box and stood on the brake. Daniel crawled up alongside him. What did Pop have in mind?

Cleopatra and Roller looked ridiculous together. Cleo's legs were much the longer, but his stride was shorter. They did not work at all well as a team. Cleo occasionally reached over to nip at Roller's ear.

They drove halfway out to the crossroads. Pop hauled to a stop. "Dan, go ride Cleo."

Daniel climbed off the wagon and onto Cleopatra's back—very carefully, because his body still ached all over. Cleopatra was accustomed to being ridden while in harness. When Daniel dragged dead trees in for firewood, he always rode while Cleo did the work. So did Pop. But although Cleo did not mind, Roller acted upset. The grulla held his head high, his ear cocked toward Daniel. The whites of his eyes showed, and when Daniel leaned over and patted him, he really got worried. Clearly, humans were supposed to ride behind, not above.

By the time they drove back into the yard,

lunch was ready. Roller no longer seemed unhappy that Daniel loomed up there above him. Pop and Daniel took another little wagon ride after lunch, doing the same thing. A few days later they drove Cleo and Roller over to Rosillas for a keg of molasses. Daniel rode Cleo all the way out and Pop rode him back. Roller did not even notice anymore.

Daniel knew what the next step was, and maybe Roller did too. A week later Pop drove Cleo and Roller toward the crossroads. Daniel rode Cleo. Halfway there, he casually stepped onto the wagon tongue and slipped onto Roller's back. You could not say Roller liked it, but a least this time Daniel was not flying through the air corral-high.

After church the next day Daniel told the whole story to Carrie, but he did not have much luck cheering her up. The Carsons would be leaving as soon as they were confident the snow was melted out of the mountains to the west and the range grass would be green for the horses. Her low spirits dampened his.

Monday after school, with Pop's help Daniel rode Roller in harness with no wagon attached. They led Cleo alongside, just to be sure. By Friday Daniel was riding with neither harness nor Cleo. Pop showed him how to teach Roller to neck-rein by crossing his reins. When he switched to a bosal, Roller had the general idea. But to the very end, Daniel owned, basically, a plow-reining horse.

Daniel thought about the fleece he had laid out, but he did not mention it to his parents. Not yet. God had given him a horse. For a while there it had looked as if Daniel would never ride Roller. Now he was riding him, but Roller was still too weak and scrawny to make the long trip to Arizona. Roller had seemed to be a sign of God's leading.

But was he?

4

Barn Fire!

Church still got boring in spots, but it was much better than it used to be. Now that Daniel had committed himself to Jesus and was reading his Bible, (not as much as he ought, but a lot more than he used to) the sermons made more sense. The hymns and prayers meant something too. In fact, because two of the songs in the hymnal were in Latin, Pastor Dougald carefully translated every word before the people started so that they would know what they were singing. Latin sounded a little like Spanish, Daniel thought.

Even Pop stayed awake now, every Sunday. Matt explained that when you commit yourself to Jesus, the Holy Spirit lives inside you and helps you understand spiritual things. Daniel thought perhaps, if that were the case, he ought to feel a lot different than he did. On the other hand, the Spirit had no body, no weight, so perhaps—it was confusing. It would all explain itself someday, Daniel was certain. His questions about God had a way of doing that.

This Sunday a box social followed church. Grace and Rachel loved box socials. Shy Naomi clung to her mother's leg and hid her face in the thick skirts. Pop pitched horseshoes with anyone who would play. Daniel went frogging with Matt and Cliff, but they did not catch anything. The weather was bleak— overcast with a suggestion of drizzle—and it matched the mood of the day very well.

Toward the end of eating, Pastor Dougald announced that the Carsons were leaving and everyone joined hands and sang "Blessed Be the Tie That Binds." The women all cried, and the men looked glum.

Daniel grew more and more restless as the afternoon got old. He wanted to go home. Home seemed like a warm, safe place. They were almost always gone most of Sunday. Why did this day feel so alien? Why did he feel uneasy? It must be because Carsons were leaving.

The Carson wagon followed the Tremain wagon as they started for home. Pop rode with Mr. Carson, and Mrs. Carson rode in the Tremain wagon with Mom. That left Daniel to drive Pop's rig with the women all talking in back. Mrs. Carson's shrill, nervous, high-pitched voice annoyed him. She was getting worse lately, talking about inane things Daniel knew Mom was not interested in—like what Mrs. Carson's sister wore at her wedding and how her cousin decided to join the navy and walked all the way to New Orleans.

They stopped at the crossroads. Pop hopped in beside Daniel, and Mrs. Carson carefully climbed down and got into her own rig. Everyone waved and said good-bye, and the Carsons took off down their road, the Tremains down theirs.

Mom sighed. "Clara should never have married a farmer. She's a city girl."

"You were a city girl, too." Pop replied. "Fanciest girl in Salem. But you changed your way of living because you decided you'd be happier changing. Clara won't change. That's her problem."

"I wish that were her only problem."

Daniel considered switching seats with Mom so she could ride beside Pop. Mostly he wished they would not talk so loudly. Sound carries easily on moist night air. Might Mrs. Carson have heard? He glanced out into the darkness where the Carson rig would be now.

Daniel hauled back on the team so hard

Caesar squealed. "Pop! Look out that way!"

"That's Carson's place!" Pop grabbed the lines out of Daniel's hands and dragged the team around fiercely. He did not backtrack to the crossroads. He sent the team at a dead run straight across country and picked up Carsons' road a quarter mile away.

A faint red glow marked the line between black land and darkening sky. The misty, murky air diffused the red until you were not quite sure it was there. Yes, you were sure. What was burning?

Grace was all set to complain about the bouncing—she even had a few words out—but she was quickly caught up in the excitement of the wild ride.

Obviously Caesar and Cleo sensed the emergency. They ran as one, in perfect rhythm. The wagon jounced so violently that the picnic hamper fell out. No one suggested going back for it. Mom clutched little Naomi close to keep her from following the hamper over the side.

The dank, drizzly air glowed brighter up ahead now. The last half mile of road straightened out, and Daniel could see the fire itself. Carsons' barn. The roof was gone. Flames howled up through the boiling smoke, the windows glowed bright yellow. As they watched, the floor of the haymow collapsed. Flames and sparks sprayed straight up through the orange smoke.

And now they were close enough to hear it. Like some infernal dragon it howled and roared, defying anyone to try to slow it down or to come near it. Burning bits of hay that had soared heavenward were returning to earth, falling all around.

It took all Pop's strength on the lines and all his weight on the brake to stop the rig. He left it just outside the farmyard gate, yelped some orders, and ran toward Carsons' house. The girls tumbled out to follow.

Mom grabbed Grace. "He said you girls stay right here! Here by the gate, and don't you go anywhere else, you hear me?"

Daniel was not "you girls." He followed Pop at a dead run.

Matt and Cliff had climbed up on the roof of their house. Mr. Carson was throwing quilts and counterpanes up to them. Six-year-old Royal stood crying in the middle of the yard. Mom grabbed him and yelled in his ear, pointing toward the gate and the girls. Grace called to him, and Royal ran for her arms and safety as fast as his stubby legs would go.

Pop came out of the springhouse with a milk pail full of water, so Daniel ran in. The cool blackness inside the little springhouse made the hot orange glow outside even more hideous. The butter tub had only a few chunks of butter in it. Daniel dumped the butter in a corner and filled the tub. Mom came bolting in with a washtub for still more water.

"To the house with that, Dan!"

"Why can't we throw it on the barn?"

"It's too late to save the barn. All we can do is try to keep the house from catching. The corncrib is burning already, and the cow shed's gone."

The cow shed! Rosita! Daniel ran outside with his tub of water. It sloshed, soaking the front of his Sunday coat. Like the barn, Rosita's shed was a hollow adobe shell with fire and smoke roaring out the top. Little licks of flame wavered in the top of the corncrib. The side of the crib facing the barn was starting to smoke.

Halfway to the house Daniel met Pop. Pop dropped his own empty pail and grabbed Daniel's tub, so Daniel picked up the pail and headed back to the springhouse. For an eternity, Daniel and his folks, Carrie and her father all hauled springwater. The spring did not produce as fast as they needed it, so Daniel got a couple of minutes' rest between runs.

The roar was a little softer now, the orange not so bright. The howling dragon was finally eating itself to death. Pop and Mr. Carson used some of the precious water trying to save the corncrib. But the fire there was too far ahead of them. Mom thought to dump some on the springhouse roof. A corner of the summer kitchen blackened and almost caught, but Carrie wet it down in time.

Matt and Cliff stayed on the roof of the house. They poured water on the spread-out bedding, keeping the roof wet all over. They kicked burning brands and hay wisps to the ground where Pop and Mr. Carson stamped them out.

Then, as if on signal, everyone quit. Mr. Carson walked out into the middle of the yard and stood there like a ninety-year-old man, his shoulders round and sagging. Pop walked over to stand beside him. Like Daniel and Carrie, Pop and Mr. Carson seemed to feel good just being together. Daniel dropped his tub and joined them. Their attentions turned from the dying barn to the flaming corncrib.

Mr. Carson spoke, his voice soft and sad and gentle. "Good thing that ain't popcorn, Ira. The yard 'd be full six feet deep now."

"Good thing it wasn't a bumper crop this year. You would've lost twice as much."

No one was laughing. It was not really joking; it was a way of hiding oneself from the smoke and smell and darkness. Daniel glanced at Mr. Carson's face. It was sooty and wet— wet with sweat and tears both.

Sobbing, Carrie pushed against her father.

He wrapped his arms around her, patting her. He pushed her face against his shoulder with a big, stubby hand. Mom was the comforter at the Tremain house. Why was Mrs. Carson not holding Carrie? Where was she when Carrie needed her?

Daniel and Mom both noticed Mrs. Carson at once. The lady stood alone in the yard, so rigid she vibrated a little. She had bunched both fists into hard knots and was squeezing them against her cheeks. She made strange, sucking, hysterical sobs. Daniel had never heard anything like it.

Mom grabbed Mrs. Carson's arm. "Why, Clara, I just remember! Our picnic hamper fell out of the wagon. Come! We must run fetch it. Hurry! Matt, come help us! Hurry!"

That was dumb, thought Daniel. *That picnic hamper fell out at least two miles back*.

Confused, Matt took his mother's other arm. The three ran out the gate into the darkness as fast as they could go.

Some minutes later Carrie had more or less pinned herself back together. Mom and Matt returned with Mrs. Carson, but they were not running. They were not even walking fast, and all were out of breath. Mom cooed something about finding it tomorrow, perhaps. Mrs. Carson looked too tired to stand up straight. The rigid shaking had ended. Spent as a wet dishtowel, Mom might have said.

Mr. Carson kissed Carrie on the forehead and left her standing there. He crossed to Mom. "Thank you, Martha," he said quietly. He wrapped his arm around Mrs. Carson and led her off toward the house with her head on his shoulder.

Daniel did not know what to do now. "Hey, uh, Carrie? I saw Zack out by the gate near our wagon. Grace caught him and tied him to the post with her sash. He must've took off running as soon as the fire started. Let's call Brunny in. She must be somewhere close around here."

"Don't bother." Carrie's voice was stricken, almost a whisper. "She's still in the barn."

"You don't know that! Come on. Let's walk the fence and try calling her in."

"I know. Her litter came Friday. She kept the pups in the loft. She would never leave them, and she couldn't have gotten them out in time, carrying them one at a time."

"Yes, but—"Daniel's voice trailed off. Brunhilde. Huge, lovable Brunhilde. "How many pups?"

"Seven. I wonder if Rosita was inside the cow shed or outside when—"

"Want me to go look?"

"No. Thanks anyway, but you needn't. It's all the same, you know." She took a deep, shuddering breath. "It's all the same."

They walked over to the porch slowly. Daniel was suddenly very tired, and Carrie looked even more tired. She sat down on the step and leaned heavily against the porch post. "Dan? Why do you think God did this to us?"

"I never thought about it. I'll think about it and let you know." That was a kind of lie. He was thinking that very thing. Why should God do this to the Carsons? And he hadn't a solitary trace of an answer.

A stalk of hay tickled Daniel's ear. He heard Lumpy mooing somewhere. He wrapped his coat closer around him. Beside him, Matt mumbled something and turned over. The hay crackled.

The fire! Daniel remembered the fire and sat bolt upright, trying to figure out where he was. It took a few minutes for his memory to push the sleep out of his head. He was in his own hayloft at home, and here were Matt and Cliff. In the house, the girls were all sleeping together. Royal was with his parents in Mom and Pop's room. And Mom and Pop were still asleep, probably, on their parlor floor. After all, there was not a single piece of dry bedding out at Carsons'.

Lumpy mooed again. It was her "feed me and milk me" call. Daniel stumbled down the ladder. Lumpy's head hung over her stanchion, wet nose high and eyes rolled back. Llorón came out of her stall and rubbed against Daniel's legs, wagging his clumsy tail. Daniel scratched his neck and belly for what seemed a respectable length of time, then grabbed the pail and milk stool. Lumpy did not let her milk down as easily for him or Pop as she did for Mom. They did not take time to talk to her.

Daniel carried the pail of warm, foamy milk up to the house. No one up. He might as well start a fire.

Fire. That barnful of hay had been Carsons' cash crop—prime hay, their source of money. All gone. The whole corn crop—what was left of it after winterfeeding—was gone. Daniel had trouble understanding the weight of it. He had no trouble at all grasping the fact that Brunhilde and Rosita were gone. Brunhilde and her pups, seven of them. Their eyes had not even been open yet. Big, bouncing Brunny; quiet, mellow old Rosita.

Daniel struck a match to the shavings and kindling in the wood stove. Flames licked up, tiny, reluctant flames. Hideous flames. Why Carsons and not Tremains? Mom was good and solid. If something like that happened here Mom would take it in stride. Poor Mrs. Carson, already so upset, was shattered by it.

To understand better how Carrie must feel,

Daniel tried to imagine his own house or barn in flames. He couldn't. He tried, at least a little, but he couldn't. He carried in more water, and he filled the woodbox to the top. He could start breakfast, but the stove was not hot enough yet. The teakettle was not even warm. Besides, he did not know the first thing about cooking.

Skirts rustled behind him. Good! Mom was up and now he could eat. No, it was Carrie. She had washed her face and hands, but her clothes were still a dirty mess, a sooty, smoky reminder of the night before. She pulled a chair over to the stove and sat down, huddled in a big shawl.

"Morning, Carrie. Why are you so cold?"

"Because your sister Rachel hogs all the covers. I woke up this morning without a stitch of blankets."

"She's not used to sharing her bed."

Carrie giggled. "Neither am I. She probably scooped up all the covers in self-defense."

"How's your mom today? You know yet?"

"I broke a solid rule in our house this morning and peeked in on them. They're both asleep. So she's all right, for now. When something's wrong, sometimes she sits up the whole night and moans. Just moans. It scares me. Can I help you with something?"

"Soon's the stove's hot you can cook, if you like. I haven't been this hungry in years."

"I see you need cooking lessons." She grinned. "All right. The first lesson when cooking breakfast is to go out to the springhouse for the bacon. The second lesson is go find some eggs. And then third—"

"All right, all right. Wanna come along?"

"Yes." Carrie stood up and rearranged the shawl. "I don't want to be alone this morning."

Carrie was always surprising him. He had three sisters, and still he did not understand girls. She could be so cheerful, open, teasing—and then some dark little comment suddenly told you how badly she was hurting underneath. They brought in the bacon and went prowling for eggs.

The overcast dampness of the night before had rolled away. All that was left was a thick, flat cloud bank off to the east. It looked almost like a smoky gray mountain range. Daniel and Carrie stepped from bright sunlight into the hen house where it was cool and very dark.

Carrie found two eggs under the runway. "Why can't chickens ever lay in the boxes you make for them?" asked Carrie.

"Just obstinate, I suppose. The whole world's obstinate."

"Isn't that the truth! Dan, did you think about that question I was asking?"

"Yeah, couldn't come up with any answer, though. Did you ask Matt?"

"It's, uh, it's not a question I want to ask him just now."

"Oh." Daniel sifted through the straw in the upper boxes. The blue-speckled hen usually buried her egg in a flurry of gleeful scratching. "Our barn is half the size of yours. Our cow gives half as much milk as Rosita and is twice as old. Our dog skedaddles at the first sniff of trouble. We ran out of corn a month ago and never did have any hay worth talking about. You lost so much, and we wouldn't have lost anything. Not really. Besides, my mom wouldn't even get very upset, and yours—Why you and not us?"

Carrie sat down on the runway and studied the chicken house floor. "Maybe it's because I asked for it. Do you always get what you pray for?"

"I sure don't, not by a long shot. But then, I don't always ask for what's best. What do you mean, you asked for it?"

Two big tears welled up, one in each eye. She sniffed. "I begged God to keep us from going to Arizona. Keep us right here where we are. I begged Him, Dan. That corn and hay were our moving money. Pa was going to deliver half the corn next week. It was sold, but he would get paid when he delivered. And with the barn gone our farm's worth half what it used to be. We can't afford to go, and we can't afford to stay. Everything is lost. The going and the staying are both lost. And all because of my selfishness."

"Oh, come on, Carrie!"

"Do you have a better explanation? I *begged* Him to make us stay!"

Daniel sighed. He sat down beside her and cupped his chin in his hands. "Gimme a minute. I don't know what the answer is, but I know what it isn't. Listen here, Carrie. God isn't going to follow the advice of some thirteen-year-old kid if He knows it will hurt someone else. And He knows."

"He answers kids' prayers."

"Sure. But He wouldn't ruin your father just because you don't want to move. False gods, they play mean tricks. Listen to all those old Greek stories. But not the true God. You can't picture Jesus doing something like that. And when you see Jesus you see the Father. He said so. No, there's some other reason your barn burned."

"I never thought of that. But then, I can't think straight right now anyway. It's all just starting to hit me."

"Besides," said Daniel, "Matt says the fleeces your father put out said you'd go. If that's what God wants, you can't buck it."

"I still have to ask God's forgiveness, then. I was asking Him to do something that wasn't

67

His will. I shoulda just accepted it."

"Mmm." Fleeces. Daniel was beginning to wish he'd never heard of such a thing. "I wish fleeces were clearer."

"Your horse?"

"Yeah, you remember. There's the dew on my fleece standing out in the corral there. Pop doesn't want to go. But my fleece says he will. And you father wants to go, but he can't."

"But our fleeces said he will. Gideon doesn't know how easy he had it."

"You said it!" Daniel stood up carefully, lest the eggs in his pockets break. "Let's try to talk your folks into staying for lunch. Maybe we can work something out, given some more time."

"Guess so." She stood up. "But it sure looks bleak right now."

Bleak. Rosita, the cow, and Brunhilde, the new mother. Hank Carson's hopes. And Roller—was he God's answer or wasn't he? Bleak.

The Carsons did stay for lunch. Mrs. Carson slept until past ten. Mr. Carson made out a list of tools he would be needing in the next week or two, and Pop and Daniel loaned him what they could. Because most of Carsons' chickens had lived in their hayloft, Mom caught a half dozen of her chickens and bound them leg-to-leg in the back of Carsons' wagon. Daniel saw her favorite blue-speckled hen among them.

Six Carsons and six Tremains filled the kitchen too full, so Mom declared lunch to be a picnic in the front yard. Picnic. Daniel thought again of Roller, who managed to show up at picnics so frequently. Was Roller their ticket to Arizona? In fact, had Mr. Carson been divinely directed, as he claimed to be? Which were Satan's suggestions and which were God's, and how did one tell the difference? Daniel sorely wished that the Christian life were simpler.

Grace managed to outtalk Mrs. Carson, telling all about Roller. Daniel let her go on. He did not feel like talking—nor listening, for that matter. Pop was quiet, too. Several times he touched the front of his shirt. Was he getting some sort of illness?

Grace took a deep breath and continued, "And then there's the time he broke loose and came over while we were eating. Two times. Only one of them, Rachel didn't close the corral gate right. And the other—"

"You mean like that?" asked Matt.

"What?" Grace's head snapped toward the yard. Daniel turned. Here came Roller at his jogging pace, rocking back and forth, ears wagging. He slowed to a halt a few feet away.

Mr. Carson shook his head. "I don't believe it."

Roller dropped his nose down near Naomi.

She batted him away. He tried Royal. Royal held out the hard-boiled egg he had just shelled. Roller lipped it up.

Even Carrie, who had been so morose all morning, started giggling.

"That nag'll eat anything that doesn't eat him first, even if it isn't horse fodder." Pop wiggled a finger toward Daniel. "Go put him back. And chase Caesar back in, while you're at it. I see him wandering out across the yard there."

Carrie hopped up. "I'll help."

It took a few minutes. Cleo was out, too, and none of them wanted to go back in. Daniel slipped the wire loop over the gate post and gave it one final, extrafirm tug. It must have been on too loosely last time, but this time it was shut and shut to stay.

As they returned to the picnic blanket, Pop was talking. "And like he said, Hank, about sowing and reaping. That sermon really got me thinking. Every farmer knows that if you sow sparingly you reap sparingly. And vice versa. But you never think to apply it to other things besides planting. It's a strong lesson."

"Agreed," said Mr. Carson. "And another thing. Like planting potatoes. You have these beautiful healthy potatoes right in your hand. You *have* them. It's the hardest thing to do, cutting them up and burying them. But if you don't, you'll never get any more potatoes."

"That's right!" said Pop. "You're taking a chance, and it's hard. Something might dig 'em up, flood 'em out, dry them up. Then you have nothing. It's a chance you take, but you take it willingly." Pop cleared his throat. "When I need a cash crop I put in cotton and expect to get cotton. Need beans, I plant beans. Well, right now, Hank, the thing I need most is money. So I best plant some if I expect to reap some, right? Now I'm just as sure as you are that it's God's calling that's sending you to Arizona. So this is to get you there."

He reached into his shirt, and from the place he had been touching off and on for an hour he brought out a brown-wrapped package, just a little one. He handed it to Mr. Carson.

Mr. Carson looked at Pop strangely, as though he knew what it was and did not dare be right. He broke the string and separated the folded paper just enough to peek inside. He stared at it a long, long minute. "Ira, you don't expect me to accept this, I hope."

"I'm hoping you will. It's greed as much as love, Hank. Like I said, I need more than I got. More than what's there, in fact. Best way to get more is plant, so in the Lord's name I'm sowing this. Martha and I talked it over and agree. And we're both certain the Lord will provide a harvest sufficient for our needs."

"But I can't begin to repay—"

71

"Don't expect you to. We're planting in the Lord's name, remember? We'll let Him pay it back. Now don't mess up our blessing by refusing it."

"Maybe a small part of it—"

"The whole thing. I don't intend to sow sparingly. Hank, it's the hardest thing in the world for us to do—financing our best friends so they can move away."

"Financing?" Mrs. Carson reached over and pulled the brown paper aside so she could see. Daniel glimpsed green—the little package was money. It had to be all the money Pop had in the world, his seed money for this spring. Pop was planting money and depending on God to give him a harvest of more!

Mr. Carson looked ready to cry, and Daniel felt embarrassed sitting there. Then he heard the now familiar plup-plup-plup, and stood up. Here came Roller again. And Daniel knew the gate had been secured firmly this time. He wrapped his belt around the little grulla to lead him back. He would just have to devise some sort of gate fastener the grulla could not figure out.

Carrie caught up with him, her eyes all wet. She was crying because she was happy, apparently—another aspect of womankind Daniel could not understand. "Isn't it wonderful, Dan?"

"I thought you didn't want to go."

"I don't mean that. Look. We're supposed to move. It looks like we can't. Then your father comes through with that money, and now we can—like the fleeces said. And since we all know that promise about sowing and reaping is true, your father stands to gain a lot more than he would otherwise. Everybody comes out 'way ahead, see?"

"Sorta. But what about my fleece? Even if Pop changed his mind—which he hasn't— now we don't have any money to move."

Carrie considered awhile. "You sure Roller is dew on your fleece? I mean, you did say, didn't you, 'If I get a horse, we're going'?"

"Sure. If God wants us to go, He provides me a horse to get there on."

"You expect this scrawny little slabsides to carry you clear to Arizona? You're growing, you know."

Daniel stared at his little grulla. "Carrie, you're right! This couldn't possibly be dew on my fleece. It's just a sort of —well, God is obviously saying, 'You can have a horse, Dan, but here in Texas.' "

Carrie sighed. "Actually, I was hoping I was wrong. I was hoping since I have to go that you'd go, too. You're the only one I can talk to about stuff like this, especially when I feel wrong about myself. Because I know you won't laugh at me or say, 'Aw, that's all right,' when it really isn't. I don't know what I'm going to do without you."

"Melanie Hawes says I'm your boyfriend."

"Melanie Hawes can stuff pickles in her ears. You're my friend. That's so much different. You know, Dan? I bet Melanie doesn't have one. A friend, I mean. She talks for two hours between breaths, but I bet she doesn't have anyone she can really *talk* to. About important things."

"And Grace," Daniel added.

"Grace?"

"Grace doesn't have someone like that, either. In fact, I can't think of anyone else in the school who does. Carrie, do you realize how lucky we two are?"

Carrie leaned on the corral rails as Daniel turned Roller in and shut the gate. "Yeah. That's why I was hoping Roller was dew on your fleece. We need each other."

Daniel nodded. That was what he had been telling God all along. Apparently the Carsons' fleeces were all sorted out, but Daniel's was surely ajumble.

5

Mr. Hostetler's Drastic Measures

Any part of April was nice. It was Daniel's favorite month. On the good years, dagger cactus* shot spikes of flowers so high in the air a man on horseback could not touch their tops. All the little cacti put out variously colored flowers, singly, in circles, and in bunches.

But that was in the good years. This April was tarnished even before it started. The Carsons left the riverbottom the last of March. April was empty. Wildflowers bloomed well only after a wet year, and last winter had been very dry. Even the daggers' efforts were half-hearted.

---

*A yucca rather than a cactus. The plant without its flower stalk reaches over six feet high.

Roller got out again and found his way into the barn. He had eaten half of all the cracked barley they owned before Daniel found him. Mr. Devlin decided Daniel must work harder if he was to finish his reader by June, so he doubled all Daniel's homework assignments. Daniel tried to bend the teeth of Mom's cultivator forward and mashed a finger so badly that he had to write left-handed for four days.

"Tarnished" was certainly the word for this April, all right, and the month was just getting started.

Friday afternoon as always, Daniel detoured through the cow pasture to say hello to Roller. He ran to the house and burst through the kitchen door. *Whanck!* "Mom? Who's been riding Roller? I said I didn't want anyone riding Roller."

"Nobody's been riding Roller, Dan. Keep your voice down and quit slamming the door. How was school today? Busy?"

"Then how come he's all sweaty? You don't get all sweaty standing around eating grass."

Over at the table, Pop put his coffee cup down and stood up. "What's he doing?"

Daniel shrugged. "Standing there. You don't get all sweaty just standing there."

Pop trotted out the door in a hurry. Daniel fell in behind. He had to jog to keep up with Pop's long-legged stride. Pop hopped the rail fence and headed straight for Roller, but the pony did not try to move away. He just stood there, head down. His position was unusual, too. His front feet were sticking out ahead of where they ought to be.

Pop pressed his fingers against the grulla's neck—taking his pulse, Daniel knew. Daniel tried on the other side but could not find it. Pop rapped his closed pocket knife against Roller's front foot. The little horse bobbed his head and tried to move away. He stumbled, terribly lame. Pop pressed his hand against the hoof and held it there, so Daniel did, too. The hoof was warm.

"What's wrong, Pop? He step on something?"

"I know what, but I sure can't figure out why. This pasture isn't rich enough. A fat pony might founder, but not skinny old Roller here. Not out here."

"Founder! That can lame a horse for life, Pop."

"That's right. He's ruint, Dan."

Ruined! "It can't be. He's our ticket to Ar—it can't be. How?"

"I said I couldn't figure it. Lots of things cause founder: fast work on hard roads sometimes; eating too much grain at once sometimes; pasture that's too thick and—why'd you just suck air in like that?"

"He got into the barley a couple days ago."

Pop sighed and started back to the house, ambling, dejected. "Well, that explains it."

"Horses recover from founder sometimes, Pop."

"If they're strong to start with. He's not. If it isn't too serious. It is. You see how he stands with his legs forward, how fast he's breathing, sweating. It all means he's hurting. His feet are so painful he can't stand on them. Best thing you can do for him, Dan, is put a bullet through his head." Pop sat on the rail fence and swung his legs over.

Daniel followed, forlorn. He stopped by the corral. "Pop, can I borrow Caesar, please? I'll be back before dark."

"Guess so."

Daniel slipped the bridle over Caesar's head, led him out, and swung aboard. Where to? His head was so muddled he could not think. He rode out toward Porksaddle for no particular reason.

Chet! He would ask Chet. Chet knew everything about everything. He would have some suggestions for saving Roller. Going the back way through Tornado Wash, Daniel was at Hollises' in twenty minutes.

"Why, hello there, Dan'l!" Mr. Hollis came walking around the end of their house as Daniel rode up. "Just in time for supper."

"Thanks, sir, but I'm supposed to get back soon. Wonder if I might talk to Chet a minute."

"He's unhitching, out in the barn."

"Thank you, sir." Daniel kicked Caesar, who was getting sluggish lately, and crossed to the barn.

Inside it was cool, dark, and musty smelling. As always, Chet had a big grin waiting for him. "H'lo, Dan. How's it going?"

"Not so good." Daniel slid off Caesar and unbuckled the crupper and girth of Chet's off horse. Daniel noticed their harness was a lot drier than Pop's. Cracked here and there, it looked older and not so well oiled. He loosened the hames and lifted the heavy harness off the mare's back. She put her nose down and shook.

Chet took the harness off Daniel's hands to hang it up. "What's wrong?"

"Roller—that little grulla, y'know?—was doing pretty good, but now he's got into the barley and foundered."

"That's bad. Happened to one of ours about five years ago. We had to put her down, she dropped her soles and lamed up so bad."

"Pop says we should, but I was hoping you knew of something to do."

Chet leaned on the rump of his off mare, deep in thought. "Hey, now! Wait. You talk to that Hostetler fellow?"

"Who?"

"Whatsisname, Abraham Hostetler. They just moved onto the Carson place. Funny accent, but he's a real good hand with horses. Cured Porter Webster's strangles."

"Porter Webster had strangles?"

"That little chestnut mare of his."

"Kinda hate going over there, but I guess I should. All right."

"How long've Carsons been gone?"

"Couple weeks. Less'n that. So that Hostetler must have moved in just right away."

"Matt told me that was one of their fleeces," Chet said. "Find a buyer for the place right away. They did."

"Mmm. Well, I best get moving if I'm going to make it home before too late. Hey, thanks, Chet."

"S'all right. Hope you can save him. He's not much to look at, but I suppose he could fatten up into a fair horse. Be prayin' for you."

"Thanks." Daniel led Caesar back out and swung aboard. Praying! In all the time since he and Pop had looked at Roller he had not once thought to pray. *Shame on you, Daniel Tremain!* And here it took Chet to remind him. So he not only had to pray about Roller, he had to ask forgiveness for forgetting about God, too. *And incidentally, God, why did this have to happen?*

For three years Carsons and Tremains had been best friends. The Carson place was as familiar to Daniel as his own. Now it was charred, disfigured so badly that it was no longer familiar. As Daniel rode in the gate he tried not to look at the barn and Rosita's cow shed. He did anyway.

He was surprised to see the mess was half cleaned up already. These people must be terrifically hard workers to get established so quickly. The corncrib, once a smoking black pile, was now a neatly raked dark spot on a neatly raked yard. The barn mess was half cleared away. Little red flags marked the corners. Apparently the Hostetlers were ready to lay the foundation for a new one already.

Daniel felt half sick about knocking on a door to be greeted by strangers. Strangers in Carsons' house. It took him a couple of moments to gather the courage even to step onto the porch.

He knocked and turned away. The sun was near the horizon already. He would never make it home by dark now. Well, he was here. He would see it through.

The door opened. "Ya?"

Daniel turned. The man was younger than Pop, shorter, and more robust. His dark blond hair stood in a thick thatch plastered down with bear grease. His full beard sported some

red hairs among the blond. Rosy red, sun-
burned cheeks bunched up into round knots as
he smiled. "Vaht can I do for you?"

"I'm Daniel Tremain. We were good friends
with Carsons."

"Oh, ya! Heinrich Carson. Beautiful family.
Come in, please!"

Daniel followed the blond gentleman into
the dining room. The Hostetlers were right in
the middle of dinner. From the far end of the
table, where Hank Carson used to sit, a lovely
lady smiled at him. She was a bit plump
(Mom's favorite word for that size was "am-
ple") with long blond hair pulled back into a
loose knot. The hair fascinated Daniel—it was
silky, soft, spun gold, the loveliest hair he had
ever seen. Three children sat around the
table—two girls smaller than Rachel and a
baby in a high seat. All had hair so blond it
was white. Would the girls have lovely gold
hair like their mother's some day?

"Katrin, kvick! Another place."

"Oh, no, sir, I can't stay. I didn't come for
dinner. I'm sorry to interrupt yours."

But the largest girl was already out in the
kitchen. Daniel heard dishes rattle.

"Vell, you haffn't eaten yet, ya?"

"But, uh—"

"So sit down, ve get acvainted. Shnitz un
nep. Not fancy, but enough."

Daniel sat down cautiously in the extra chair Mr. Hostetler dragged forward. What was a nep, and was it edible? The stuff surely smelled good. The hospitality here was just as warm as it had been with the Carsons. Daniel felt a bit guilty feeling so comfortable among these people who had replaced his friends.

Big bowls were plunked down in front of him. There certainly was enough. The main dish of apples and salt pork with dumplings was indeed fancy.

"Can ve do for you, or are you chust visiting?"

"A friend of mine, Chet Hollis—tall, red-haired, lives over east of here—says you're a good hand with horses. My gelding foundered, and I was hoping you might have some advice."

"Founder." Mr. Hostetler's bushy blond brows puckered. "Oh, ya. Laminitis." He shook his head. "You-shly, they never kvite get over it. How bad?"

"Pop says bad. He's really hurting."

"How long?"

"Noticed it this evening."

"Goot. Not too long. Vhere you liff?"

"Well, first you take the road south to the forks—"

"I know. After supper you make a map. Tomorrow by dawn maybe I come by and look at him, ya?"

"I don't mean for you to go clear—I mean, it takes a couple hours."

"Happy to for neighbors." The gentleman mopped up the last of the gravy on his plate with his cornbread. "Two hours, eh? Little faster under saddle I t'ink, ya?" He chuckled. "In Prussia, you ride two hours, you leave the state. Maybe two states. Here you chust so reach your neighbor's house. Ve haf long time getting used to distance here. Texas ferry big. Ferry big."

"Yeah. Pop says Texas consists of miles and miles of miles and miles."

Mr. Hostetler considered that very seriously for a moment. Suddenly he burst into a raucous laugh. He rattled off something in a foreign language to his wife, and she laughed, too. She asked something and Mr. Hostetler translated. Daniel spent ten solid minutes answering their questions about his family and asking about theirs. He was surprised to hear that Katrin was older than Rachel—she was a head shorter.

Now he would be able to tell Pop about the Carsons' replacements. They were Mennonites from Prussia, just come to this country. And suddenly he found himself explaining all about Roller's possibilities as a sign and the perplexities of the whole thing.

Mr. Hostetler sat nodding, chewing, ruminating. "Dis fleece business. Gideon. Ya, I understand dat. Goot idea. Not the best, but goot."

"What do you mean, 'not the best'?"

"Vell, fleece ting ferry nice. But not de best vay to know vaht God vants." He paused again, translating in his head. "You see, fleece answers little qvestions. But mostly, you do vaht God vants by reading de Bible. Over und over. Den you know vaht God vants because you know Him like a person. Don't haff to t'ink about it so much, see?"

Daniel sat thinking about that. Mr. Hostetler had a very good point there. Daniel had been leaning too much on fleeces and not enough on just plain learning about God. Suddenly it did not matter so much whether Roller was a sign or not. With all those other things taking up time, Daniel had been neglecting his Bible. Mr. Hostetler was right—more right than he realized, no doubt. Daniel had better get back to basics and quit worrying so much about fleeces.

It was nearly dark outside. Mom said you must never just eat and run. How could he excuse himself politely? He followed Mr. Hostetler's example and cleaned up the last of his gravy with the last of his cornbread. Mrs. Hostetler certainly was a fine cook!

Mrs. Hostetler poured coffee. Daniel put lots of milk in his. Coffee with milk tasted better than tea with milk. He glanced out the window again. No barn shadow darkened the yard. It looked so bright and open for this time of night.

"Oh, look!" said Mr. Hostetler. "Is almost dark, and you haf all dat vay to ride yet. Ve should not haf kept you so late." He said something to his Katrin, and she brought a pencil and several old envelopes. Mr. Hostetler drew some diagrams, Daniel drew a map, then everyone was shaking hands, and Daniel was sitting on Caesar headed home—all so quickly.

There was a light in the barn as Daniel rode into the yard. Who would be doing chores this late? He slid off and led Caesar into the barn.

The lamp was hung by the box stall in the corner. Pop stuck his head up over the rail. He did not bother with hello. "Home by dark, huh?"

"Sorry. Stopped by Chet's, and he said talk to Mr. Hostetler, so I did. That's where I've been."

"Who's Hostetler?"

"Carsons' place. He showed me some things to try tonight. You brought Roller in."

"He can barely walk. If a cat or a pack of coyotes come on him out there, he'd be a dead goose. I was thinking of putting him down before you got back. Should've."

Daniel hung over the stall rail. His little horse looked worse than when he had first seen him. The spark was gone from his eye again, the nose hung low. He stood motionless, rocked back on his heels. The nostrils still flared, and he was so wet that Pop had thrown a blanket over him. His breath came in rapid little snorts. Maybe Pop was right. Maybe they should just—

Daniel fished a bit of paper from his pocket. "Mr. Hostetler didn't know the word for it, so he drew a picture. He says we ought to try this if it's only his front feet." He showed Pop the sketch of a sling. "And put his front feet in a bucket of cold water."

"How long?"

"About an hour. For the water. The sling thing all night."

"Guess we can't lose much more than sleep. Let's try it."

Daniel dragged down the big soap-making tub as Pop threw a rope over a rafter. The other end he anchored somewhere in the loft. Together they tied the ends of Pop's old army blanket into the rope and passed it under Roller's belly. Pop hauled on the rafter line, and the blanket rose up, snug under the horse.

"He says not clear off his feet. Just enough

87

to take some pressure off, Pop."

Pop knew something about slinging a horse. Still, it was a trickier operation than Daniel would have guessed. Daniel slipped the tub under the horse's front feet and hauled cold water until it was half full. The little grulla felt too miserable to fight the sling or kick at the tub. After a few minutes, Roller's breathing slowed a little.

A tiny flicker of hope lightened the blackness of Daniel's heart. The worst was still to come. The little horse would get sicker before he got better. Pop said that a couple times (perhaps thinking that Daniel had not heard it the first time). But hope is hope. Daniel grabbed it, held onto it—nearly strangled that bit of hope, he clung to it so tightly.

When they finally returned to the house, Daniel went straight to bed, worn out. But he could not sleep. He kept arguing with himself.

"You're so hung up on fleeces, you're working it backward. The only reason you want Roller to recover is so you'll go to Arizona."

"That's not true, Daniel Tremain! I want Roller well for his own sake."

"Selfish Daniel! You're not thinking of Roller at all."

"I am too!"

Mom poked Daniel awake at dawn. Mr. Hostetler had just arrived. He must have left home with first light. Daniel peeked out at the man's horse before he came downstairs. It was obviously old, a bit arthritic. But didn't it look sleek and well cared for! Not too fat, nor thin—and it sidled about like a three-year-old. Mr. Hostetler, like Pop, did not own a saddle. He rode with his plow bridle, the reins a length of clothesline rope.

Mom insisted Mr. Hostetler have some breakfast first, especially since Pop was still sitting down. Daniel was not hungry. He ate something, though, for politeness. Mr. Hostetler and Pop were friends at once, talking, questioning, laughing. He spoke Russian (Ukrainian, specifically, he said), German, and English. And now he must learn Spanish, he said, if he were to make do in Texas. He reminded Daniel very much of Matt. No challenge seemed to daunt him.

Finally Pop was finishing his coffee. The whole family followed Mr. Hostetler out to the barn. He approved the sling with a nod, tapped Roller's hooves gently, considered Roller's pulse as Pop had done. He wagged his head sadly.

He laid his hand on a back foot. "See? He got little in back feet, lots in front feet. Bad. Are you villing to get drastic?"

"How drastic?" Pop asked.

"Ve drench him and bleed him. Den you

must soak his feet in cold vater four times each day. And ven he can valk, take him to the river wit' moving vater. It vork maybe."

The bit of hope faded and slipped through Daniel's grasping fingers. Pop had said, "Not a penny of money, not a minute of time." Daniel could not do all that. He had to go to school.

"Uh, Pop? S'pose I could skip school a week or so?"

"Not a day." Mom put an end to that idea in a hurry just with her tone of voice.

Pop looked Daniel in the eye. Daniel turned away. He was too near tears. "Guess we can manage," said Pop. "Soaking his feet, I mean, not skipping school."

The hope flickered up again. Daniel was beginning to feel like a bouncing rubber ball—up and down and up and down.

"Goot. I happen to brought some tings." Mr. Hostetler gave the girls a packet of tan powder and set them to mixing a bucket of medicine. He gave long and careful directions. It all sounded important and complicated, and Daniel could not see the use of a lot of it—making sure you stir it ten whole minutes, for instance. As soon as the girls left for the house, Mr. Hostetler pulled out a packet with a strange steel blade.

"Dis is not for little girls to vatch. Ve finish before dey get back maybe."

90

He felt along Roller's throat, pushed on his neck. A vein bulged beneath the ragged brown coat. With his mysterious blade, Mr. Hostetler cut quickly, deftly. Dark blood—almost black blood—spurted. Pop was right there catching it with a bucket.

Daniel felt clammy, dizzy. The sour in his stomach boiled up into his throat. Afraid he would fall, he turned around and sat down, his back to the men. Mom did not say anything, but she reached a warm, soft hand down and pressed his head against her leg. He felt grateful.

"Ya goot! You a goot horse, Roller! Goot horse. Now ve must take him a little valk. Help me wit' dis ting."

Daniel heard the rope grating across the rafter, and he stood up. Pop was bringing the sling down. Except that Mr. Hostetler was pressing his fingers hard against the place he had cut, there was nothing to suggest what had just happened. Daniel did not look toward the bucket. Pop picked it up and carried it outside.

Mr. Hostetler walked alongside as Daniel led Roller out into the morning sun. The pony did seem a bit perkier. He stumbled, lame yet, but he did not seem to mind moving so much.

The girls came running out with the vilest gruel Daniel had ever seen.

"Ah! Chust in time!" Mr. Hostetler grinned.

Right, Daniel thought. *Your timing was just great.*

Pop dug the drenching funnel out of the toolshed. They put the medicine down Roller. Mom forced one more cup of coffee and piece of pie on Mr. Hostetler. He left instructions just like a doctor and rode off home.

Daniel soaked Roller's feet as specified, an hour at a time four or five times a day. He stayed home from church next day just to keep the schedule. Monday morning as he and the girls headed off to school, he saw Pop coming out of the springhouse with a bucket of cold water.

He not only owed Pop a dollar for the horse, he now owed Pop time as well. But then, he had learned a lesson from the whole affair. Handy as a fleece might seem, it was no substitute for knowing God's Word inside out and using it as your guide.

In fact, he was getting sick of fleeces.

6

Chet Disappears

May arrived every bit as dry as April had
been. Ranchers wagged their heads sadly and
drove their stock closer to the river. Half the
tinajas* in the hill country were dried up, they
said. Wesmorton's yearling steers trampled
Pop's cotton because he could not afford fenc-
ing. No one intended it to happen—it just did.

Roller now stood straight on his legs. Apparently he had recovered, but his weight had fallen off again. He still looked too feeble to walk
all the way across the yard. Reluctantly, Daniel
asked around here and there. Would anyone
like to buy a potentially nice horse for one dollar? Everyone smiled politely or responded
with a joke.

The talk of the county, though, was the new
_____
*Tee-NAH-hah—a natural pothole where water collects.

Hostetler family. Talked funny, and the missus just learning English, but they were sure all-right folks—everyone said so. Daniel was proud to say he knew them personally. And, having met them, he could really snicker at some of the wild rumors circulating about them.

Mr. Hostetler himself, however, said that had the Carson farm sold for the full price with barn intact, he could never have afforded to buy it. The Carsons' misfortune was his blessing. It had made possible his moving into this fine area. Now his friend Jacob Enns—Jake had the money to pay full price for a good place. In fact, Jake was looking for a farm in this area. But the Hostetler family and the Carson spread were tailor-made for each other.

Daniel made mental note to write all that to Carrie, just as soon as she sent him her address. She could quit worrying about any ill winds her prayers might have raised.

The first Wednesday in May, Daniel and the girls arrived home from school just as Chet's brother Bart rode into their yard. Bart was overweight and undersmart, Chet claimed. Actually, Daniel knew Bart was smart enough—just lazy. And his horse, Birdbrain, was even lazier. Daniel had ridden Birdbrain once—the most uncomfortable horse he had ever sat on—and he did not care to do so again.

"Hi, Bart. Sorry you missed school today. You would have loved the spelldown. What can we do you for?"

"Came to get Chet."

"Chet's here? Great! He must be inside. Come on in."

As Daniel led the way, Bart grumbled behind him. "Chet's gonna be in a pile of trouble for this. Pa expected him home long afore now."

"How's school today?" Mom paused with her sewing. "Hello, Bart."

"H'lo, ma'am. Came to fetch Chet."

Mom looked perplexed. "I haven't seen him. Did he say he was coming here?"

"No'm. Didn't say where he was going atall. Took his gun, so we opine he's out hunting javelina. He's been gone so long we figured he musta come visiting."

"When did he leave home, Bart?"

"Day afore yesterday."

"And he's not back yet?" Daniel exploded.

"Abe Hostetler's raising his barn tomorrow," said Mom. "Did you try there?"

"Tried there first."

"Tornado gone?"

"Sure. Chet don't go nowhere except on that horse."

Tornado and his rifle were all Chet owned. And Chet had been considering leaving home. Just quitting and leaving. Would he do it with-

95

out at least letting his ma know? Daniel thought not. Chet cared about his ma.

"Which way did he leave, do you know?"

Bart shrugged.

"You didn't try to track him?"

"Chet's the tracker at our place."

Daniel caught his mother's eye and held it. She scowled and shook her head. "I don't know what you could do at Hollises' anyway, Dan. Unless Chet shows up or sends some word back. Besides, your father needs Caesar and Cleo both tomorrow over at Hostetler's."

"Mom, I can't just sit around here. I can take Roller."

"Are you sure he's ready to ride?"

"If he isn't—" Daniel did not want to think about that. "If he isn't, Chet owes me a dollar."

Daniel grabbed some cookies and went out to catch Roller. As he swung aboard, he whistled for Llorón. "Come along, hound. We might need you."

Barton and Daniel, despite their horses, made it to Hollises' in twenty-five minutes.

Chet's pa was sitting in his usual place, the rocking chair on their porch. He lurched back and forth, back and forth, staring straight ahead with bleary eyes. He had been crying, obviously. Chet's ma came running out on the porch as Bart and Daniel clattered up.

She stopped cold, and her face fell. "Oh.

96

Good to see you, Dan'l."

"Evening, ma'am. Mr. Hollis. Sorry I'm not who you were expecting. So he hasn't come back yet."

Chet's pa grunted. "And he ain't gonna. He's run off. Took his gun and run off somewheres. I smelt this coming a long time. Ever since Margaret left he's been restless. He's run off."

"Did he leave any note? A letter?"

Ma shook her head. "Looked all over for one, hoping—"

"His Bible still here?"

Barton scowled at him. "Chet don't own no Bible."

"He does too. Red edges. Did he take it along?"

Ma turned and scrurried into the house. Daniel followed. He heard Bart shuffling in behind him. They found the Bible in Chet's room under his pillow.

Ma stared at Daniel. "I didn't even know he had one."

"So he hasn't run off, or he would have taken it with him. I was kind of hoping we wouldn't find it. It would be easier to believe he's safe, that way."

Chet's pa loomed in the doorway and sagged against the doorpost, that vacant, glassy look still in his eye. Chet's ma plopped down on his bed and sat there studying the floor. One little tear hesitated on the rim of her eye, then dived down her cheek. "Six kids. We had six kids, Dan'l. One born dead, two died when they was babies. And Margaret and Chet and Barton. I loved them babies, even the stillborn. She was such a pretty little thing.

"Margaret's gone, working in town. She's a maid at the hotel there, she says. Ain't seen her since she got the job. And now Chet—if he's gone and dead, I don't know what I'll do. I love my kids, Dan'l, all six of 'm."

What do you say to a grieving mother? "Yes'm. And Chet loves you back."

"Does he? Margaret don't. She hasn't been to visit once since she left. She's forgot us. Shed us, and glad of it. And now Chet—"

Daniel hunkered down nearby, the better to be able to see her face. "I just thought of a thing this minute that I never thought of before. That must be just how God feels. He loves every single person, but almost all people don't love Him back. He loves you more than you love your kids. I guess it really must hurt Him when He doesn't get loved in return. Same as us."

There was no argument in her voice, no defiance. Just sadness. "If God loves me, Dan'l, why is He picking off my kids? They're all I got."

"Lotsa things we don't know. I don't know why God does a lot of the stuff He does. But I do know He loves us, and He does what's best for those who love Him. And Chet loves Him—he told me so—so God will do what's best for Chet. Won't let him down—"

"You mean He's keeping my Chet safe?"

"He's keeping Chet, whether Chet's alive or dead. That's even better, least from Chet's point of view." Daniel was so nervous talking like this that his voice shook a little. "Mrs. Hollis, last month or two in town, when I first got Roller, I was talking to Chet. He was thinking about leaving home, but he didn't want to leave you. You needed him, he said. And most of all he was worried because you and his pa aren't saved. He loves you."

"He said that?"

"Yes'm. You don't know Jesus, and it weighs heavy on him."

"I don't believe you!" Chet's pa rumbled from the doorway.

Chet's ma snapped her head around and shouted at him. "You hush, Pa! This here boy tells the truth, and you know it. If he says so, it's what Chet said, and I believe him. You're the one kept telling Chet not to talk religion around here. Said you didn't want to hear his fanatical talk, kept shutting him up whenever he tried to talk about Jesus.

"Now Chet's gone, and God alone knows where. He might be hurt or—dead, or—" She clouded up again. Suddenly her voice turned firm. She had decided something. "Clay, there's only one thing Chet ever asked us for. One thing in his whole life. Well, you and me we're gonna do it and right now. Whether he's alive or dead this minute, he's gonna get the only thing he ever asked us for. Come 'ere. Get down on your knees here right aside of me."

Chet's ma came down off the edge of Chet's bed and plunked down. She bawled at Chet's pa again. "Right now! Get down here!"

Daniel was not only embarrassed, he was also confused. To his great relief for once he remembered to pray before he opened his mouth. He asked God to take over the whole situation, because Daniel surely did not know what to say or do.

Chet's pa looked more embarrassed by far than Daniel felt. He hesitated, opened his mouth to object several times, and shut it again. He shuffled over and clunked down onto bony knees beside his wife. She grabbed his hands, both of them (*probably to keep him from walking out,* Daniel thought).

She nodded. "I heard about being saved, Dan'l, but never understood about it. You have to tell us what to do. You know. Like Chet wants."

100

"Well, uh—" Daniel got down on his knees, too—partly because kneeling was a good position in which to pray and partly so that Chet's pa would not feel so embarrassed. "First you repent. That means you recognize you're a sinner and decide down inside that you'll do your best to keep from sinning anymore. You ask God to forgive all your sins—the things you've done wrong—and He does. He promises He'll forgive you if you just ask Him. Then you ask Him to put Jesus in your heart."

"That's all?"

"It's easy to say, but you have to really mean it. Every word. Bible says if you truly believe that Jesus paid for your sin and came back from the dead, and if you right out and say so, you're saved."

"Do you have to understand all that exactly?"

"Not to start with. Later, though. And understanding is easier later, because you have the Holy Spirit to help out. And another thing. Chet can't save you, and neither can I. God has to do it."

Mrs. Hollis's voice stumbled at first, uncertain. But Daniel could see her sort of filling up with confidence and something else, too. Joy? Relief? She prayed it all to God—the repentance, the forgiveness, Jesus

As worried as he was about Chet, Daniel felt

the happy flow, too. Joy. That's exactly what it was. This was the one thing Chet had wanted most—to see his parents saved as he was. And it was happening. Even more important, this was what God wanted. Suddenly Daniel understood why Chet was gone. This would never have happened under less trying circumstances. God had a purpose in "picking off" Mrs. Hollis's children. He could not have reached her any other way.

Chet's ma did not have to prod Mr. Hollis too much to persuade him to make the same commitment. And Barton, watching from a corner of the room, had no choice. She got him down on his knees, too.

Daniel opened Chet's Bible to John—as good a place as any for them to start reading—and marked it with an envelope from the dresser. Although the sun was nearly down now, he would have to go. And he could not go home. He would rest until the moon rose, then try tracking Chet.

Chet's ma gave him a pot of beans and a full canteen. She slung them in a blanket across Roller's withers. Chet's pa owned hounds, but they were lion hounds. Even if they started out on Chet's trail, they could not be trusted to stay with it. Should they cross a lion track, they would leave Chet to chase lions.

Was Llorón any good? He was, after all, a

hound. But he was also untrained as far as people-tracking went. Ah, well, Llorón was all Daniel had. He stuck Tornado's curry brush and Chet's worn sock in Llorón's face. He led the hound in a wide circle out around the farm. With the brush and sock he reminded Llorón a couple of times that they were seeking Chet. Was this the way he should be going about it? He had not the slightest idea.

With a loud and sudden bugle call, Llorón dropped his head and trotted off. Daniel swung aboard Roller. Behind him he heard Chet's pa cheering. "Listen to 'm! That hound's got it! Got it solid, too!"

The dog was onto something's scent solidly, all right. He loped forward with cheerful determination. But was the scent Chet's?

7

Roller Finds
a Picnic

Along the riverbottom, April was springtime.
Summer came instantly with May. The
wildflowers disappeared overnight. Dried-up
prickly stalks marked where some had been
just a few days before; others had no
tombstone at all. Short green grass turned yellow, bleached. The little pepperweed under the
bushes shriveled to scratchy little skeletons.
And the sun beat down as hot as on any summer day.

It must be noon—the sun was nearly over-
head. Daniel had slept a few hours between
sundown and moonrise, but they had been
traveling most of the night. Llorón would lose

the trail now and then, circle and find it again. Daniel had scooped out a few handfuls of beans at dusk and given some to Llorón. He ate a few more at dawn. But he wanted to use his beans sparingly. Who knew how long they would be out?

Daniel hurt, especially where his legs joined his body. He rode with knees up, legs down, slouched, scooted forward, scooted back. There was no comfortable position on his bony little horse's narrow back. The insides of his legs were so tired they quivered every time he raised his knees. He could feel a sore rubbed raw where his tailbone ended. He had no hat. His eyes burned, half blind, because there was no shade and no protective brim.

Llorón lost the track again. He circled. He circled wider, looking almost frustrated. Daniel called him in. Daniel had a very general idea which way home might be. But basically he was lost. Alien country stretched away from him in all directions. There were no familiar landmarks to make him feel better.

He tied Roller to a woody, dead-looking bush and sat down on the hot caliche.* Llorón flopped down beside him, panting. The dog was tired. The horse must be tired, too, but he looked neither more nor less bedraggled than

---

*Kah-LEE-chee—Hard, sun-baked ground with a clay base, common in deserts.

when they had started out. How had the scrawny beast managed this far?

Daniel scooped out a handful of beans for Llorón. They felt slimy and looked grayish. He sniffed them. Spoiled. Rotten. The canteen was nearly empty. Daniel gave Llorón a few laps of water out of the palm of his hand and drained the last of it.

Well, God, now what? No food. No water. Lost. It must be a hundred degrees in the sun and no shade around. No Chet. Soon there will be no horse. Roller surely can't keep going much longer. Daniel felt awfully, terribly alone.

No, he should not feel alone. After all, Jesus said He would never leave or forsake him. On the other hand, Jesus also had said, "Where two or three are gathered, there am I," and Daniel was only one. Christians dehydrated and died in this desert heat just as quickly as did any unrepentant sinner.

What if Chet were home safe now, and Daniel were the one to die alone out here? It was a distinct possibility, and Daniel was too weary to be frightened by it.

Sorry to dump this mess on you, God. Especially when I did it again—forgot to pray when I started out. I just took off without asking You, and now here I am. You're going to have to take care of Chet and me both—and this old hound and this stupid horse—we're at the end

107

of our rope, all of us.

Daniel stretched out with his head in the shade of a straggly little yucca. Well, most of his head—the shade patch was too small to cover his chin. He closed his burning eyes.

He heard a thin crackle. Poor old Roller was so starved he was browsing on that dead old bush he was tied to. The tired horse kicked pebbles as he dragged his feet.

Dragged his feet? Daniel sat upright. His grulla had bitten off the branch he was tied to. Now he was headed away, shifting into that easy, rolling pace, up the low bajada.†

"Roller, come back here! Roller!" Daniel hauled himself to his feet and started running. If Roller got away—Daniel slowed to a stumbling walk. This whole thing was unreal. *When life starts to seem unreal, it means you are dying of thirst.* He had heard that somewhere.

Here he was in the middle of nowhere, staggering along behind Roller. And yet he saw up the bajada beyond Roller a picnic spread out under a scrubby little mesquite. An army blanket, it looked like—grey or green. He had not noticed, but obviously Roller had. *Stupid horse.*

Daniel was almost there before he realized what the "picnic" really was.

†Buh-HA-da—the gently sloping skirts at the base of desert mountains.

"Chet! Hey, it's you! Hey, Chet!" Daniel broke into a lumbering run. He dropped down on the blanket beside his red-headed friend, so out of breath he could not talk in a straight line. Salt-sweat in his eyes blinded him.

"Chet, you—you all right?" Daniel gulped in a few more hot breaths. "No, you aren't. Chet?" Daniel poked him. Chet opened his eyes and looked at him—no, he looked past him—and did not see a thing. He did not even recognize Daniel! His face, which tended to redden in the heat anyway, was a frightening, shiny, cherry red. His lips were cracked— cracked, chapped, and encircled with a ragged brown line. Mom called it a fever line.

Daniel was so horror-struck by his friend's face that it was a few moments before he noticed Chet's right arm. Thick and swollen, it filled his sleeve like feathers fill a pillow. Daniel tugged the cuff up a little way. The arm was purple and gray, with green casts here and there. What could possibly—

Snakebite. That was what. Daniel had never seen a real case of snakebite. But little x's of dried blood showed him where Chet had cut himself, to try to suck the poison out. It had not worked, apparently. Daniel suddenly felt sick. He probably would have lost everything, had he anything down there to lose.

That hopeless, empty feeling of a few moments ago was nothing compared to the emptiness that emptied him now. Chet was dying right in front of him. If only he had not drained his canteen. If only his horse were stronger. If only he knew a quick way home. If only Llorón—where was Llorón?

Daniel called him. Nothing. He called again, louder. He whistled. Moments later he heard scratching and rattling far up the bajada. The happy hound came bounding down across the stones and swarmed, jubilant, into Daniel's lap. His whole face was wet. He had been drinking water!

"Llorón, where'd you get that?" Daniel retrieved his empty canteen and scrambled up the slope. Llorón had come down this way, so this must be the most direct route. He struggled a quarter mile at least, getting more and more worried the farther he left Chet behind. Finally, in a wrinkle in the slope, green willow peeked out. Willows live with their feet in water. Daniel started noticing tracks—tracks of coyotes, jackrabbits, cottontops.‡ Faint game trails laced in and out amongst each other.

Daniel reached the willows and climbed twenty feet beyond. He pushed aside dense, knee-high shrubs. There it was, just a small seep in a crease in the rocks. Daniel scooped aside a sloppy mixture of watercress, algae,

‡Cottontop—A small gray quail with white head.

110

and bees. By mashing his canteen into the puddle, he could just about half fill it. A bee got sucked into it, so he poured out the water and started over. *Can't have Chet drinking bees.*

He would bring Roller up and get more water later. He would wash out and fill the bean pot, too. He ran back down the slope to Chet. No matter that the water was so far away. They had water.

Daniel settled down beside Chet and trickled water a few drops at a time onto Chet's tongue. Long minutes passed before he woke up enough to take a proper drink. Finally Daniel left him briefly to take Roller up to the seep. The thirsty horse drained it. Daniel tied him and left him there. The seep would refill, and Roller would drink again. Daniel was not needed.

Toward evening Chet woke up enough to talk. His mind still wandered in and out, but at least he recognized Daniel now. And his red face was no longer so vivid.

"Dan, there's a seep back that draw a ways. Used to be."

"Still is. You're drinking part of it."

"You found it. Good."

"Llorón found it. Tell me what happened to you."

Chet sighed. "Reckon I don't know near as much about the Bible as I thought I did. When

111

I spread this blanket out to eat lunch I scared up a rattler under the bush here. Just a little one. Well, sir, before I left home I'd just been reading the gospel of Mark. And at the very end of it Jesus said if you're a believer you're immune to snakebite, remember? So I tried it out. Grabbed that snake about in the middle. Dan, he hit me so hard I could hear his mouth slap me."

"You grabbed a rattler on purpose?"

"Jesus *said*, Dan! Tornado took off like a shot when I hollered. And he had my canteen on his saddle. My arm started burning right away, so I knew I'd got a wallop. I tried putting a tourniquet on it, but the sticks kept breaking. Best I could do was hold it tight in my hand. Wasn't very tight. By the time I decided I better try to find that seep—if it wasn't dried up, that is—I was too sick and dizzy to walk. And scairt. Dan, Jesus *said* it wouldn't hurt me! Guess I ain't a true believer after all."

Daniel folded his arms across his knees to make a chin rest. "Lemme get this together. I can't believe you'd really—Chet, that's the dumbest thing I ever heard of in my whole life."

"Then how come He said that? And you're supposed to test whether what God says is true, aren't you?"

"Testing God. Hold on." Daniel's mind was

spinning too fast to think clearly. It took him a while to sort things out and line them up properly. No matter. They certainly were not in any hurry just now. "Pastor Dougald was talking about testing God, but that was months ago. Matt and I looked the references up, but I can't remember them."

Chet's left arm was finally well enough coordinated for him to get a drink himself. The sun had dropped down behind the hills above them. Everything felt refreshingly cool.

"All right, Chet, now listen. To put out a fleece is one thing. You're asking God a question. But tempting Him—"

"But—"

"Don't but. Listen. Tail end of the book of Acts: Paul was putting wood on a fire when a snake came out and bit him. He shook it off, and everyone sat around waiting for him to swell up. But he was fine. So you see, Jesus' promise works when you really need it. What *you* were doing was exactly what Satan told Jesus to do. When He was being tempted, one of the temptations was to jump off the pinnacle of the Temple. A steeple sort of thing, I suppose. Remember?"

"Yeah, I read that. Somewheres in Matthew, I think."

"I don't remember what Jesus said exactly. Something like, 'You shall not tempt the Lord

113

your God.' Jesus could have jumped, too. But it would have been tempting God. Challenging Him for no good reason. So although Jesus could have, He didn't. See?"

"I was listening to the devil, right?"

"Sorta. Don't feel all alone. Everybody does now and then, even if you don't mean to."

"That temptation," said Chet. "Satan quoted Scripture, same as Jesus."

"Sure. Satan knows Scripture. But he just uses the parts that are handy. You read one line—a promise—but didn't remember all the other places in the Bible that help explain it. Like Mr. Hostetler said, the best way to do what God wants is to know Him better by reading all of Scripture."

"Then you don't make stupid mistakes like I did—"

"As often," Daniel corrected.

"Hit's a good lesson to me. Too late, but a good lesson."

"Why too late?"

"You don't think I'm gonna live this one through, do you? The black and blue is clear up to my shoulder almost. And I feel—well, I feel myself dying inside, Dan. Dan? Do you think I really am a believer? Safe?"

"Sure. You believed what Jesus said without any doubts atall. You made a mistake, but it was a believing mistake. In fact, you wouldn't have made it if you didn't believe."

Chet broke into a wide, happy grin. "That's right! I never thought of that. So I belong to Him after all."

Daniel stood up. "Do you know the way back?"

"Yeah. We're about twenty miles from Springer right now, and home is off that way."

"Springer! That's great!"

"Dan, I can't—"

"We're gonna take off, now that it's cool. Ride double as far as we can get, rest until moonrise. I did that last night, and it works pretty good."

"But I can't—"

"It's better than lying around here. Besides, I'm lost. I need you to get us back, and you need me to get you to a doctor. So if Roller doesn't drop over, we'll both get out of this in one piece."

Daniel stopped. Now why did he say that? He was supposed to be cheering Chet up, making him confident. Chet knew how feeble Roller looked. A fine cheerer-upper he was!

Chet's blanket helped a little to pad out Roller's sharp back. Daniel boosted Chet on and swung up behind him. He could more easily keep Chet on that way. Roller walked awhile, ambled along at the easy rolling pace awhile, walked again. They traveled until it was too dark to see, then rested. Roller's nose nearly touched the ground. When the moon slipped up over the hills they were on their way again.

Daniel expected Roller to buckle beneath them any moment. When the grulla started stumbling badly, Daniel got off and walked. But he had too much trouble keeping Chet from slipping. He climbed back on. Besides, riding was faster. The night was lasting forever.

Barking dogs announced Springer a quarter mile before they reached the first buildings. As Daniel hopped up onto the doctor's moon-washed front porch to pound on the door, a clock inside chimed four.

Daniel should have rested Roller all day, at least, but he knew how Chet's ma must feel. At first light he was on his way again. He arrived at Hollises' a bit past breakfast time.

Tornado, still caked with dust and dry sweat, stood forlorn in the corral. Daniel was glad— he had been hoping the little horse would make it home all right. He had always liked Tornado.

Daniel explained to the Hollises where Chet was, how long he would probably stay there, and what the doctor had said. He did not tell how Chet came to be bitten. Let Chet tell them that if he cared to. Then he pushed Roller on the last short distance home. Chet's ma must not be the only mother worried.

When Daniel arrived at the corral he knew best, Roller's nose hung no lower than it had in the beginning. He had carried two men twenty miles and had gone all that distance with no feed and little water. And he looked no more ready to drop than when they had started—or no less. Here was the toughest little horse Daniel had ever known.

And he owned it!

"Mail, M's. Tremain! Mailman. You got a letter." The postman's voice was right outside the kitchen window.

Pop put down his fork. "I didn't even hear him ride up."

But Mom was already out the door. Daniel shoved the last of his beans onto his fork with one finger while no one was looking. Grace scowled across at him. Grace never missed a thing.

Mom's voice came bubbling up onto the back porch. "A drink of lemonade, at least. I squeezed some fresh this morning. Please come in."

Mr. Carpenter appeared in the kitchen door and grinned at Pop. "H'lo, Ira. You're looking good."

"Yourself, too, George. Sit down, sit down. Martha offered you lunch?"

"Yep. But I ate at Hostetlers'. Thanks anyway." Mr. Carpenter plunked down in the chair beside Daniel. A little gray cloud of dust rose off his pants. June was even drier than April or May.

"Didn't mean to interrupt your lunch here —"

"No bother. Heard anything about Chet Hollis?" asked Pop.

"Doin' better, doin' better. Doctor says that was a close one. Y'know what his ma is saying? Hit was prayer. She sat down and started praying and just kept it up till he was safe (heh heh). Silly, but that's what she says."

Pop looked at him levelly. "I don't doubt a minute that's what saved Chet. Too many strange things happened but what God's hand was in the matter, start to finish."

"Uh, right. Of course." Mr. Carpenter cleared his throat. Mom set a tall glass of lemonade before him, and he drank half of it the first tip up. "Dee-licious, M's. Tremain."

Mom plopped down and buried herself in her letter. Daniel took his plate to the sideboard and refilled Mr. Carpenter's glass. Lemonade was dripping where the mailman's moustache crept down over his upper lip.

"If you want that answered, M's. Tremain, I'll stay until you get your letter wrote. Save you a trip to town."

Mom was absorbed in the letter. She glanced

up absently at her name. "Answer? Oh, no. No, thank you, George, I'll not answer it just now. It's from Hank and Clara, Ira. The Carsons are about halfway there. They had to rest the horses a week in New Mexico. Hank says Clara is as fit and cheerful as when they were first married. Says it's doing wonders for her, this moving. And the children are fine. Send their greetings."

Pop nodded. "I suppose they won't know what kind of address they'll have until they get there."

"Hank says they'll let us know right away." Mom went back to the letter, rereading. Her eyes were misty. Daniel glanced over at Pop. He was studying her, his lips a tight, thin line. Thinking. Pop's mouth always made a thin line when he was thinking hard.

Mr. Carpenter finished his lemonade, and Pop went with him out to his horse. When he came back inside, Mom was still staring at her letter, her lip a bit quivery. Daniel knew how she felt. He missed the Carsons almost as much as she did.

Pop stood against the back of her chair and rubbed her shoulders. She leaned her head back against his leg.

He tickled her cheek a little. "Want to go?"

She nodded, almost ready to cry.

"Start packing then. Dan, come help me.

Axles have needed greasing for a month. Now's as good a time as any."

Mom sat upright. "Ira, do you know what you just said?"

Pop nodded. "I was talking to that friend of Hostetler's, that Jake Enns. At the barn raising. Abe spoke highly of our place here, and Enns is willing to buy if we're willing to sell. Guess the Ennses and the Hostetlers would like to live fairly close to each other. Price is good. Real good. That seed money we planted on Carsons would reap a good return."

"Oh, Ira—" Mom really started crying now—from happiness, apparently. Carrie was constantly doing that, too. Daniel would never figure out women.

Pop went outside. Daniel followed.

Arizona! Just like that. Pop did not make decisions without thinking everything through, so he must have been thinking about this for quite some time.

Daniel felt ashamed about his fleece. Here he had refused to believe God when he got what he asked for. He had even tried to manipulate God instead of getting to know Him better.

Everything was coming out exactly as Daniel and Carrie had hoped. And yet—Daniel looked around the familiar yard, over toward the chicken house and forward toward the barn. Roller stood inside the corral near the fence, flicking flies, half asleep. This was home. Illinois was not home. Arizona certainly was not home. Suddenly Daniel dreaded leaving this friendly, familiar, dusty little farm. He wanted to go. But he did not want to go. No wonder he could not figure out women. He could not even figure out himself.

Daniel was halfway across the yard when Chet's pa came driving up in their rebuilt buckboard. Chet sat beside him, thin and a little pale but just as cheerful as ever. He gave Daniel a big grin.

"Light off there and set a spell," Pop offered.

"Can't stay, Ira, thanks. Just stopped by on the way up from Rosillas. Dan'l, boy, broughtcha somethin'."

"Sir?" Daniel looked from Chet's pa to Chet and back. Chet was grinning broadly.

Chet's pa fished around under the buckboard seat and brought out a corked brown bottle. "Hit's whiskey, boy, case you don' recognize it."

"Yes, sir. But I don't—I mean—and neither does Pop—"

"That's right! And since May, neither do I. No more. That there's my last bottle. Thought you might like the pleasure of pouring it out in the dirt."

Would he! Daniel eventually won his struggle with the cork. It popped out, and he turned the bottle over. Judging by the smell that drifted up from the warm fluid, Daniel could not imagine anyone wanting to drink the stuff.

Pop laughed out loud. "Clay, this is the best news I've heard in ages!"

"You should see ma, Dan." Chet hesitated. "She looks ten years younger. But then, when my folks came into Springer to fetch me home, she looked ten years older. Been a rough spring in some ways. Just great in others."

"Amen!" boomed Chet's pa. "Gotta go. Chet here still tires out easy. Heat gets to 'im."

"You all right otherwise?" asked Daniel.

Chet shrugged. "Chunk gone outta my arm, just eaten right out. And my hand's a little numb in spots. Doctor says it always will be. The lesson's worth the price, I reckon. I mean, with Ma and Pa knowing Jesus. Wouldn't a happened elsewise."

Chet's pa nodded. "Lord sure works in strange ways, don't 'e? Well, gotta go. Later." He dragged his horses' heads around. Chet and Daniel waved, and they were gone.

Pop spread a piece of wagon canvas out on the ground to keep dirt out of the hubs. He threw a rope up over the hay davit. As they raised the wagon off its left wheels, Pop said, "You didn't mention about Arizona."

"Chet's pa seems so happy right now—

more lively, you know? And we got more or less bad news. So I thought I'd ride over there in a couple days and tell Chet then. Think that's all right, Pop?"

"Sounds good."

"Why'd you decide to go? Miss Carsons?"

"A little. Mostly, I got thinking. The reason for staying was that we're started here. But what do we have, exactly? Not much. Not much at all. Can't be any worse in Arizona, and it just might be better."

Daniel heard a strange gritching sound over at the corral. He and Pop turned together to look.

A brassy nose was poking at the wire loop holding the corral gate shut.

"Well, I'll be hanged," said Pop. "I pushed that down snug, too."

The wire loop jiggled, slipped upward, and fell away. A grulla head pushed the gate out a few inches. The gate shuddered as grulla shoulders shoved it open. Roller stepped out into freedom, walked over, and stood near Daniel.

"The canvas, Pop! You laid out that piece of canvas to grease the hubs on. That means 'picnic' to Roller."

Roller thrust his long bony face into Daniel's stomach and nuzzled Daniel's pockets.

After all, when you come to a picnic, you expect to be fed.